Starting
with Alice

Books by Phyllis Reynolds Naylor

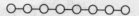

SHILOH BOOKS
Shiloh
Shiloh Season
Saving Shiloh

THE ALICE BOOKS

Starting with Alice
Alice in Blunderland
Lovingly Alice
The Agony of Alice
Alice in Rapture, Sort of
Reluctantly Alice
All But Alice
Alice in April
Alice In-Between
Alice the Brave

Alice in Lace
Outrageously Alice
Achingly Alice
Alice on the Outside
The Grooming of Alice
Alice Alone
Simply Alice
Patiently Alice
Including Alice
Alice on Her Way

THE BERNIE MAGRUDER BOOKS
Bernie Magruder and the Case of the Big Stink
Bernie Magruder and the Disappearing Bodies
Bernie Magruder and the Haunted Hotel
Bernie Magruder and the Drive-thru Funeral Parlor
Bernie Magruder and the Bus Station Blowup
Bernie Magruder and the Pirate's Treasure
Bernie Magruder and the Parachute Peril
Bernie Magruder and the Bats in the Belfry

THE CAT PACK MYSTERIES
The Grand Escape
The Healing of Texas Jake
Carlotta's Kittens
Polo's Mother

THE WITCH BOOKS
Witch's Sister
Witch Water
The Witch Herself
The Witch's Eye
Witch Weed
The Witch Returns

THE YORK TRILOGY
Shadows on the Wall
Faces in the Water
Footprints at the Window

PICTURE BOOKS
King of the Playground
The Boy with the Helium Head
Old Sadie and the Christmas Bear
Keeping a Christmas Secret
Ducks Disappearing
I Can't Take You Anywhere
Sweet Strawberries
Please DO Feed the Bears

BOOKS FOR YOUNG READERS
Josie's Troubles
How Lazy Can You Get?
All Because I'm Older
Maudie in the Middle
One of the Third Grade Thonkers

BOOKS FOR MIDDLE READERS
Walking Through the Dark
How I Came to Be a Writer
Eddie, Incorporated
The Solomon System
The Keeper
Beetles, Lightly Toasted
The Fear Place
Being Danny's Dog
Danny's Desert Rats
Walker's Crossing

BOOKS FOR OLDER READERS
A String of Chances
Night Cry
The Dark of the Tunnel
The Year of the Gopher
Send No Blessings
Ice
Sang Spell
Jade Green
Blizzard's Wake

Starting

with Alice

Phyllis Reynolds Naylor

Aladdin Paperbacks
NEW YORK · LONDON · TORONTO · SYDNEY

First Aladdin Paperbacks edition March 2004
Copyright © 2002 by Phyllis Reynolds Naylor

ALADDIN PAPERBACKS
An imprint of Simon & Schuster Children's Publishing Division
1230 Avenue of the Americas, New York, New York 10020

Also available in an Atheneum Books for Young Readers hardcover edition.
Designed by Ann Sullivan
The text of this book was set in Berkeley Old Style.
Manufactured in the United States of America
10 9 8 7 6 5 4 3

The Library of Congress has cataloged the hardcover edition as follows:
Naylor, Phyllis Reynolds.
Starting with Alice / Phyllis Reynolds Naylor.—1st ed.
p.cm
Summary: After she, her older brother, and their father move from Chicago to Maryland, Alice has trouble fitting in her new third-grade class, but with the help of some new friends and her own unique outlook, she survives.
ISBN-13: 978-0-689-84395-2 ISBN-10: 0-689-84395-X (hc)
[1. Single-parent families—Fiction. 2. Family life—Fiction. 3. Friendship—Fiction. 4.Schools—Fiction.] I. Title.
PZ7.N24 Sq 2002
[Fic]—dc21 2001053610
ISBN-13: 978-1-4169-3685-5 ISBN-10: 1-4169-3685-8 (Aladdin pbk.)

To Sophia,
with more to come

Contents

No More Barbies

Here's what I love:
  Alice, my name
  Pepperoni pizza
  Felt-tipped pens, sixty-four colors
  Snow
  Flip-flops with sequins on them
  Books about girls like me
  My dad

Here's what I hate:
  Anything with gravy
  Lint in my belly button
  Brussels sprouts
  Lester's smelly socks
  Washing my hair

Splinters
Barbie dolls

When I was in first grade back in Chicago, I got three Barbie dolls on my birthday. It wasn't so bad then because I didn't have any at all.

One Barbie came with a beach bag, another came with a wedding dress. The third one came on a motorcycle. My dad said why didn't I keep the ones with the beach bag and the wedding dress, and give the motorcycle Barbie to the poor children.

"Where will we find some poor children?" I asked.

"I don't know," said Dad, "but I'll start looking."

Now that we've moved to Maryland, some of the kids at school think *we're* poor. Dad and my brother, Lester, and I live in this little two-bedroom house in Takoma Park. Dad has one of the bedrooms, I have the other, and Lester, who's fifteen, gets the whole basement to himself so he can play his guitar, his saxophone, and his drums.

Here's what I have:
    A purple beanbag chair
    Three Barbies
    A birthstone ring
    A panda-bear purse

Seventy-one books
Bubble bath
Green sparkle nail polish

Here's what I don't have:
Pierced ears
My own house key
Levi's jeans
Really long hair
A pet
Ice skates
A mother

When I was in second grade, I got my fourth Barbie, only she died a horrible death. It was Lester who taught me to hate her. That Barbie came with a sports car, and Lester said why didn't I keep the car and ditch the doll.

"What's the matter with her?" I asked.

"She's a freak," said Lester.

"She is not!" I said.

"Look at her neck!" said my brother. "Look at her legs! She looks like she's been stretched! No girl looks like that."

I turned Barbie around and around on the table and looked her over. Her long yellow hair came halfway down her back. She had big breasts and skinny arms and a perfect face. There's another thing I don't have: breasts.

I went in the bathroom with Barbie and took off all my clothes except my underpants. Holding Barbie in one hand, I looked at us together in the long mirror on the back of the door.

My hair is sort of strawberry blond and it barely touches my shoulders. My neck and legs aren't long, my arms aren't exactly skinny, and though my face is okay, it's definitely not perfect.

I looked at Barbie again and thought of flushing her down the toilet, except she would probably stop it up.

I put my clothes back on and went out to the living room. I twisted Barbie's head until it was facing backward. I bent one of her legs back until it was touching her nose, and bent the other foreward until her foot was over her head.

"What are you trying to do, Alice? Kill her?" Lester asked as he came in eating a cheese sandwich. Lester looks a lot like pictures of my dad when he was younger. His hair is dark, and there is just a shadow of a mustache above his upper lip.

"I don't think I like Barbie anymore," I said.

"How come?"

"Just what you said; she's a freak," I told him.

Lester looked down at the Barbie in my lap. "She wouldn't be so bad if she didn't look so stretched and skinny," he said. "Probably nothing wrong with her that a little scrunching up wouldn't cure."

"How?" I asked.

Lester picked up the Barbie, and we took her to Dad's workbench in the basement. He turned the handle on Dad's vise until the two metal parts separated far enough that we could squeeze Barbie in between them. Her head was at one end, her feet at the other.

Then Lester began to turn the handle the other way. The two metal pieces moved closer together, squeezing Barbie tighter and tighter.

"Uh-oh!" said Lester as Barbie's head began to bend backward, and suddenly it snapped off. Barbie fell to the floor, and her head rolled under the basement stairs.

"Lester!" I said. "You killed her!" I was trying not to laugh.

"I didn't mean to do *that!*" he said. "I thought it would scrunch her up a little."

Dad came down in the basement to get the garden hose. I had just picked up Barbie's body and Lester was on his hands and knees under the stairs, looking for her head.

"What's this?" asked Dad.

"The operation was not a success and the patient died," Lester said, getting up with Barbie's head in his hand.

Dad had a strange look on his face. A worried look. He stared at Lester and then at me. "You seem to think it's funny," he told us.

It was, but I don't know why. I could see that Lester was trying not to laugh too.

"So what will it be next?" Dad said. "Pulling wings off butterflies? Setting little puppies on fire?"

I couldn't believe what he said. Lester and I would never do anything like that, ever!

"No more Barbies," said Dad. "No more Barbies in this house." He picked up the hose and went upstairs.

I looked at Lester. He grinned.

"Yay!" I cheered. "No more Barbies!"

"No more freak show," said Lester, and handed her head to me.

I took her back upstairs, fastened her head on with double-sided tape, and put her in her sports car. I sent the sports car whizzing off the edge of the coffee table. Barbie lost her head again.

Next I put her on the motorcycle and ran her off the back of the couch. This time her head went down the heat register on the floor. I guess it rolled all the way to the furnace. Even I didn't like to think what was happening to Barbie then. I put the rest of her in a cracker box and buried her in our backyard.

Lester came in later and found her sports car upside down under the coffee table.

"So where's the freak?" he asked.

"Buried," I said.

"We could probably fix her up if you really wanted," he told me.

"Not without a head," I said. "Besides, I'd rather have a friend. Somebody I can talk to, I mean."

"Good thinking," said Lester. "Welcome to the real world."

I never got another Barbie after that, so there were no more Barbies for the poor children.

2

Donald Sheavers

Lester told me once that Dad worries about whether he's raising us right. That's why he gets upset sometimes. My mom died when I was four or five, I can't remember which. I guess I was in kindergarten. We were living in Chicago then, and for a while my Aunt Sally took care of us.

It's weird when you lose your mother. Weird and sad. For a long time I could remember the smell of her skin—the hand lotion she used. But as we were packing to leave Chicago for our move to Takoma Park, I realized I couldn't remember that smell at all. I cried more then, because I couldn't remember her smell, than I'd cried at her funeral.

In fact, I think I only cried a little at the funeral. Everyone else around me was crying, but I kept thinking, *She'll be okay when she wakes up.* I didn't know about *forever.*

The reason we moved from Illinois to Maryland was because my dad—Ben McKinley—was promoted to manager of a music store. It's called the Melody Inn. Dad plays the piano, the violin, and the flute. He sings, too. He said my mom liked to sing, especially songs from *Showboat.* Maybe that's why they fell in love, because he heard her sing.

I can't sing at all. I can say the words, but I can't tell if my voice is going up or down. It used to be that whenever there was a party and we sang "Happy Birthday," everyone looked at me and said, "*Al-ice!*" and laughed. So now when I go to birthday parties, I just move my lips.

Aunt Sally didn't like to see us leave Chicago. Her daughter, Carol, had told us that Aunt Sally's afraid Dad will marry on the rebound.

"What's the rebound?" I'd asked Carol. Carol's two years older than Lester.

"That's when a man loses someone he loves and marries the next person who comes along," she had said.

The day we moved to Takoma Park, the first woman who came along was a neighbor, Mrs. Sheavers, who brought over a lemon cake. The cake was good, but her voice was too loud and she talked too fast. When she finally went home, I said to Dad, "Please don't marry Mrs. Sheavers."

"What?" said Dad.

"Just don't marry her on the rebound," I said.

He laughed. "Alice, she's already married. She's got a child."

I was glad to hear it. "Well, promise me you won't marry the first woman who comes along," I said.

"Believe me, I'm not thinking about marriage right now," he said.

I didn't know whether this was good or not. My Uncle Charlie was getting married in November, and he was fifty-seven. So if it could happen to Uncle Charlie, it could happen to Dad. I really, really wanted a mother, but I sure didn't want Mrs. Sheavers.

Carol had also told me that Aunt Sally was afraid that Lester would fall in with a bad crowd if we moved away, and that none of us would eat right. Dad must have been worried about Lester and me too when we moved, because he started thinking right away about finding us some friends.

"I can make my own friends, Dad," Lester said. "Please don't start arranging my life."

Lester hadn't wanted to move at all, because he was a sophomore in high school and he'd have to leave his girlfriend. When he first found out we were moving, he wouldn't speak to Dad for a week. He said that Dad had ruined his life and that we might as well be moving to Siberia, because who ever heard of Maryland?

"You've heard of the Baltimore Orioles, haven't you?" Dad had asked him. "You've heard of Johns Hopkins University and the Chesapeake Bay?"

But Lester said the Baltimore Orioles stunk and he didn't care about John Hopkins. All he cared about was Amy Miller, this girl he'd leave behind. But then he found out that Amy Miller kissed his best friend in the backseat of a Toyota, so he broke up with her two days before we left, and then he said we couldn't get to Maryland fast enough. After that, everything was okay.

After we finished Mrs. Sheavers's cake, though, Dad washed the plate and asked me to take it back and to thank her very much.

"If she's not there, just give it to Donald," he said.

"Who's Donald?" I asked.

"Her son. Didn't I tell you?"

"You didn't say it was a *boy!*" I complained. "I don't want to make friends with a boy."

"All you have to do is hand him the plate, Alice," said Dad. "It wouldn't hurt you to say hi."

I trudged across the grass to the house next door, but I didn't have to ring the bell because Donald Sheavers was sitting at the top of the front steps eating peanuts out of a bowl and throwing the shells on the grass.

He was probably one of the best-looking boys I'd ever seen. He had really white teeth and brown hair and blue eyes. He looked like the Barbie doll's boyfriend, Ken.

"Here's your plate," I said. "It was really good."

"What? The plate?" Donald said, and laughed. I wished he'd just take it so I could go back home, but he went on eating peanuts.

"Tell your mother we liked it very much," I said, holding it out in my hands.

But he still didn't take the plate, so I just set it on the step beside him.

"I like chocolate better," he said. "What's your favorite?"

I shrugged. "Chocolate, I guess."

"Are you Alice?" he asked.

"Yes."

I started to leave, but he said, "Do you want to see something no one has ever seen before and no one will ever see again?"

I stopped and looked at him for a minute. I couldn't think of anything he could have that no one had ever seen before and would never see again.

"Okay. What?" I said.

He held up a peanut, broke open the shell, and took out the nut. "No one has ever seen this nut before," he said, popping it into his mouth and swallowing, "and no one will ever see it again."

I couldn't tell if Donald was stupid or smart. "Everyone knows that," I said.

"You didn't," he said, and grinned. "Want one?" He held out the bowl.

I didn't, especially, but I decided to stick around long enough to see if he was dumb or what. "What grade will you be in?" I said, sitting down and breaking open my peanut.

"Third."

"So will I," I said. "Do you know what teacher we'll get?"

"It'll be either a man or a woman," said Donald.

Now I *really* couldn't tell if he was stupid or just mouthing off. "What's nine times seven?" I asked.

"Same as seven times nine," said Donald.

"I'm going home," I told him.

"Want me to come over sometime?" he asked.

"I don't know," I said. "Maybe." It would have sounded rude to say no.

"Where's your mother? I haven't seen any mother over there," he said.

"She died."

"Oh," said Donald.

"Where's your dad?" I asked in return.

"He doesn't live here anymore. He's in Denver," said Donald.

"Well, my dad's not marrying on the rebound," I said quickly, in case he got any ideas.

"What's a rebound?"

"The first woman who comes along," I said.

"Well, that's good, because if your dad married my mom, you'd have to be my sister," said Donald.

That thought was just too awful for words. "I've already got a brother," I told him.

"How old?"

"Fifteen. He'll be sixteen next week."

"When I'm sixteen, I'm going to get my learner's permit and drive a car," said Donald.

"Good for you," I said, and ate another peanut.

"You want to see our dog?" he asked.

"Sure."

Donald got up and walked to the front door. He opened the screen and called, "Come on, Killer!"

I jumped up and braced myself, because I hadn't been around animals much. I waited. Nothing happened. I wondered if this was going to be the dog no one had ever seen before and would never see again.

But then I heard the click of a dog's toenails on the floor inside, and out came a dog so old, it must have been somebody's grandfather. It was sort of dirty white with long hair that covered its eyes. It came out as far as the doormat and then stopped.

Donald took his foot and gently nudged Killer's hind legs until he moved out a little more so Donald could close the screen.

"Here's Killer," he said.

"How old is he?" I asked.

"Almost a hundred, in dog years. Mom's had him forever."

I knelt down and put out my hand, but Killer didn't even turn in my direction.

"Is he blind?" I asked.

"Almost."

"Why don't you trim the hair over his eyes, then?"

"Because it's been that way since he was born, and if we trimmed it now, the light would hurt his eyes."

I didn't know whether to believe that or not.

"Is he deaf?" I asked.

"Probably."

"Why did you name him Killer?"

"Because Mom read an article about robbers. It said if you put a dog's dish outside your house with the name 'Killer' on it, robbers will think twice about breaking in. So after Dad left, we changed Muffin's name to Killer."

I went over and patted Killer on the head. He turned

and sniffed my hand, and his tail gave a little wag. "His nose still works," I said.

"Yeah, he's got a good nose," said Donald.

"Well, I've got to go home," I said. "I'll see you at school."

"Yeah," said Donald.

When I got back, Dad said, "I see you made a friend." I knew he'd been watching us from the window.

"He's not a friend. He's a neighbor," I said. "I want some girlfriends."

"You'll find some," said Dad. "In the meantime, at least you have Donald."

I still had a peanut in my hand, so I went in the living room, where Lester was reading a magazine.

"Do you want to see something no one has ever seen before and will never see again?" I asked him.

"Yeah?" he said. "What?"

I held up the peanut. I broke open the shell and took out the nut. "No one has ever seen this peanut before," I said, and popped it into my mouth, "and no one will ever see it aga—"

I made the mistake of trying to swallow as I said the last word, though, and choked. I coughed, and suddenly the peanut came back up and shot across the floor.

"Wrong!" said Lester.

3

The Terrible Triplets

At least I had someone to walk with on the first day of school. Dad had already registered me, but he asked if I wanted him to go along. I tried to think how it would look if I showed up for class with my father.

"I don't think so," I said. "I'll walk with Donald." I didn't have much choice, because Donald was standing at the back door with his nose pressed against the screen, watching me finish my Cocoa Puffs.

"Okay, if you're sure," Dad said. "It's good that it's only two blocks away."

I brushed my teeth, got my backpack, and went out to walk with Donald. He had a faint gray smudge on his nose from pressing it against our screen door.

"Dad said our teacher was Mrs. Burstin," I told

Donald as we walked around to the front of the house and started down the block.

"She had a baby last year," he said.

"She did? Then I guess she's got somebody to take care of it," I said.

"Or else she ate it," said Donald.

I stopped on the sidewalk and stared at him. My dad wanted me to be friends with *this boy? "What?"* I said.

"Some animals eat their young," Donald said, grinning.

"You're really weird, Donald," I told him.

"You can't leave lion cubs alone with the male lion for a minute or he mauls them," Donald went on.

"Don't you ever talk normal?" I said.

"What do you want to talk about?" he asked.

"Anything except this," I answered.

The closer we got to school, though, the noisier it got, and we didn't really have to talk about anything. I watched to see what other girls were wearing. I guess I didn't look too different, except that a lot of the girls were wearing thin glass bead bracelets on their arms. I wished I had a bead bracelet just then.

Donald suddenly saw some boys he knew and gave an earsplitting bellow before he cut across the playground and ran to join them.

I just kept walking along the sidewalk, but when I got to the school driveway where I had to cross, a large patrol girl, with socks bunched around her ankles, held up the palm of her hand and I had to wait. She went out in the middle of the driveway to move the orange traffic cones so that a school bus, far down the street, could pull in.

But the bus was behind a line of cars that were all stopping to let kids out. I could have gone across the driveway and back eleven times before that bus got there, but each time I shifted my feet, the big girl came over and stuck the palm of her hand within two inches of my face.

Finally the bus pulled in. By this time there were six more kids standing beside me, all wanting to cross. We figured she'd let us go, but now she saw a bus coming from the other direction. It, too, was behind a line of cars that were stopping to let people out.

A boy next to me started to cross anyway, but the patrol girl blew her whistle and put her hand against his face. She leered at us when she did it. The very first girl I met on the first day of school, and I didn't like her at all.

When we finally got to cross, I looked around for Donald, hoping he'd come over and talk to me, but he was running around the monkey bars. This time, though, he was all by himself. Maybe all the whooping and hollering he'd been doing before was to make it seem as if he knew everybody on the playground.

Maybe even people who had grown up right here in Takoma Park didn't have a million friends either. I went over to the front entrance and sat down on the steps.

Three girls came by. They were sort of dancing along the concrete, their arms across each other's shoulders, singing a silly song like they were in a TV commercial. Like they were triplets or something. They each had glass bead bracelets on their arms, and one of them had pierced ears. They must have known I was watching them, because when they got right in front of me, they sang even louder, looking my way. I just reached down and tied my shoe.

But I wondered if that would ever be me, laughing with two best friends, our arms around each other. I decided right then that this would be perfect—two best friends, so that if one was busy, I could still do something with the other, and all three of us would get together for birthday parties and after school. By the time the bell rang and we lined up to go inside, I decided that my first job in third grade would be to make two best friends.

Mrs. Burstin was a thin, wiry-looking woman with metal-rimmed glasses and very curly hair. She smiled at each of us when she called our names. The three girls who had danced by me on the playground were Megan, Dawn, and Jody, and they were all in my class.

"I'm going to let you choose your own desks," Mrs.

Burstin said, "but it will be up to you as to whether you're allowed to keep them for the rest of the year. So you may sit with friends to begin with, but if this proves to be a problem, then I'll assign your seats myself."

She had hardly finished talking when kids began scurrying across the room, changing seats, calling out to each other. I was sitting in the second row and didn't know anyone except Donald, so I just stayed where I was, Donald behind me. But Megan and Jody scrambled to save an empty seat near them for Dawn, and she skidded when she went to sit down and missed, landing on the floor.

All three of them shrieked with laughter. It really was funny, so I laughed too. But they looked at me as though this was their own private joke and I wasn't included. I didn't laugh any more.

The big thing in third grade is the multiplication tables. We'd already learned our twos and fives and tens in second grade, but now we had to learn our numbers all the way up to twelve times twelve, Mrs. Burstin told us.

Not only that, but we would be learning the names of the states and their capitals, and their time zones and principal products. We would memorize the presidents and have a field trip to the Capitol, and sometime during the year, we would be tested in reading and arithmetic. I could see right away that I was going to be a lot busier in third grade than I'd ever been back in second.

Was all this necessary? I wondered. When I was forty years old, would it matter if I knew what eleven times twelve equaled or what the major products of Nebraska were?

I was hoping that Donald would eat with me at lunchtime so I wouldn't have to eat alone, but the boys gathered at one end of the lunchroom and the girls at the other.

I'd brought my lunch so I wouldn't have to worry about how things worked when you bought one. I sat down at one end of the table where Megan and Dawn and Jody were eating. Jody turned and looked at me, and then she faced her friends again and they went right on talking.

A girl with dirty hair came and sat across from me. "Hi," she said.

Jody and Dawn and Megan looked at the girl and giggled.

"Hi," I said, staring down at my peanut butter sand-wich.

The girl with the dirty hair didn't say any more either. She was eating a little packet of potato chips, and she chewed with her mouth open. I couldn't look.

Four more girls squeezed in at our table. One didn't

talk at all, one talked all the time, the third one laughed at everything the second girl said, and the fourth one got sick and had to go to the nurse. She'd just made it out into the hall before she threw up.

"Euuuuew!" everyone went, so she threw up again.

In the afternoon Mrs. Burstin handed out maps of the United States with each state outlined in black, but without a name. Our homework was to fill in all the names of the states along with their capitals and their principal products.

"If you don't have a map of the United States at home, you might look in an encyclopedia or a road atlas. There are many places where you can find all of the states," Mrs. Burstin said. "We have fifteen minutes before the bell, so you may begin, and you're welcome to use any book in this classroom."

I found a map in the front of our geography book and started in. The first state I looked up was Illinois. The second state I found was Maryland. They were very far apart. I hadn't known they were that far away from each other, halfway across the country. And suddenly I wanted so much to be back in Chicago near Aunt Sally and Uncle Milt and Carol.

I wanted to stand by Aunt Sally in the kitchen and make Christmas cookies, and read the comics with Uncle Milt, and help Carol blow-dry her hair. I didn't want to be in Takoma Park with the Terrible Triplets sitting on one side of me and the girl with the dirty hair across from me at lunch; I didn't want to live next to Donald Sheavers and his stupid dog.

I didn't even wait for Donald when school was over that day. I hurried outside and sneaked across the driveway when the patrol girl with the saggy socks wasn't looking.

"Hey!" I heard her yell as I walked on down the sidewalk. I didn't even turn around.

In Montgomery County, high school begins a lot earlier in the morning than elementary school and it gets out earlier in the afternoon, so Lester was already home. He was out in the kitchen eating pretzels and drinking Mountain Dew. He swallowed in big gulps, and his Adam's apple moved up and down.

I just plopped down in a chair across from him and reached for a handful of pretzels.

"So?" he said. "How was it?"

"It stunk," I said.

"How come?"

"Nobody's friendly and Donald's dumb," I said. "And the only girl who talked to me chews with her mouth open."

"Yeah?" said Lester. "So do you."

I immediately pressed my lips together and promised myself that I would never, ever eat like the girl with the dirty hair.

"Did anybody talk to you?" I asked Lester finally.

"Yeah, a couple of kids. I met a girl who was really friendly. It might not be too bad," Lester said. "Cheer up. It's only your first day."

I went to the living room and sprawled out in my purple beanbag chair. What I was really missing right then, I think, was my mother. If I had a mother, she'd come in and talk to me and maybe brush my hair back from my forehead and make me a special dessert. Or maybe we'd go to the mall and she'd buy me a bead bracelet. Or we'd go to a park and feed ducks.

Dad came home early from the Melody Inn. I was still in the beanbag chair with a half-finished map of the United States on my lap and my geography book open beside me. This was a dumb assignment.

"I don't care about soybeans," I said to Dad. "I don't care about timber."

"Well," he said, "sometimes it's not so much *what* we learn that's important as the fact that we're training our minds to connect things and remember."

"I remember when I used to help Aunt Sally bake Christmas cookies," I said.

That made my father look sad. "I don't think so, Alice," he said. "I believe that was your mother. Don't you remember? You always stood on a chair at the table around Christmas and helped your mother bake cookies."

I do that a lot, I guess. Get my memories all mixed

up. I don't care about the multiplication tables; I wish I remembered more about my mother.

That night, just before I turned out the light, I took her picture off the dresser and sat down on the foot of my bed. She was wearing a blue dress with white buttons, and she was holding me. I was probably about one and a half in the picture. Somebody must have been making silly faces at me because I was laughing at the camera. Playing with the buttons on my mother's dress and laughing. Mother, though, was looking at me and smiling. It's the best picture we have of my mother and me, but I wasn't even paying attention.

4

Oatmeal

Friday night, Dad was late for dinner. Because he's the manager, he often stays late, but he usually calls when he does. This time Lester and I had made macaroni and cheese and heated a can of green beans, but when Dad hadn't come home by six-thirty, we ate without him.

Whenever I think about something happening to my dad, though, I get a stomachache. Once you've lost a parent, I guess, it's sort of like losing an eye. You can't help but think what would happen if you lost the other one.

"Where's Dad?" I asked in this small voice I get just before I cry.

Lester was reading the sports page at his side of the table. "Working late, that's all," he said, not even looking up.

Now my voice was shaking. "Well, why hasn't he called?"

Lester looked over at me. "Something probably came up at the store. When you're the manager, it's easy to lose track of the time." He studied me some more. "If you're really worried, go call him."

I got up from the table and dialed the Melody Inn. The phone rang and rang. Nobody answered. I came back and sat down across from Lester. I tried to imagine what would happen to us if Dad had got in an accident or something and Lester had to raise me himself.

"Can you cook anything besides macaroni and cheese?" I asked.

"Bacon-and-tomato sandwiches," Lester said, and went on reading.

I thought of the things Aunt Sally cooked that I liked. "Do you know how to make pot roast?" I asked.

"No."

"Strawberry pie?"

"Alice, I'm trying to read," Lester said.

I leaned back in my chair and played with my green beans. I turned one to the left and the next to the right, all around the edge of my plate. "I know how to use the washing machine," I said.

"Good for you," said Lester.

"But I can't iron shirts."

"Al, will you please shut up and let me finish this article?" Lester said.

Just then I heard a car door slam, and a minute later, Dad's footsteps on the porch. I was so glad to hear him, and at the same time I was angry at him for making me worry.

"Where *were* you?" I bellowed as soon as he came in the door. And then I stopped, because he was holding a pillowcase in his arms, and it was moving as though it were alive.

"I had a little errand to do and it took longer than I thought," he said.

A high, desperate wail came from inside the pillowcase. Dad knelt down and opened the end, and out came a little gray-and-white kitten. Its fur looked exactly like a bowl of oatmeal with cream showing through in places.

"Oh, Dad!" I cried, and knelt down beside the kitten. "Is it ours?"

"If you want it to be."

It had a little pink nose and tiny red mouth. When it opened its mouth and mewed, I could see its pink tongue, and then it wobbled over to me, one paw in front of the other, and leaned against my leg, mewing again.

"Oh, it's beautiful!" I said. "So *tiny!*"

Dad was smiling. "One of the clerks at the store had a cat with kittens, and she's been trying to find homes for them. I drove out to her house in Olney to pick it up."

I gathered the kitten in my arms. It was as light as a Kleenex. Hardly weighed anything. It squirmed and mewed again until I stroked it under its chin, and then it started to purr.

I took it over to Lester. "Isn't she *cute?*" I said.

"How do you know it's a she?" he said.

I stared at the kitten.

"Look underneath," said Lester.

I held the kitten up, but all I could see was fur. I handed her to Lester. He looked. "It's a she," he said, and gave it back. "Good grief! Another girl in the family!"

Dad smiled and came over to the table to eat the cold macaroni. The green beans were cold too. He dished both up on a plate and put them in the microwave. "She's probably hungry. Janice sent some food along. The kitten's been weaned from her mother, so she doesn't need milk, but you'll have to feed her several times a day and make sure she has water."

"Who's Janice?" I asked.

"One of the clerks. Our best clerk, actually."

"And don't forget the litter box," said Lester.

"That's right. There's a plastic box in my trunk with a bag of litter. Bring those in, will you, Lester?"

He grunted and got up from the table. "Where do you want me to put it? How about Al's room?"

We decided on a corner of the kitchen for the food and water dish, and the little alcove by the back door for the litter box. I wanted to call the kitten Oatmeal, and Dad said that was a good name. Lester said I could call it anything I wanted as long as he didn't have to take care of it.

I spent all evening playing with Oatmeal. I sat on the floor and let her crawl into my lap. I took a long string and dragged it along the floor, while Oatmeal hunkered down, her eyes huge, and then pounced. I put a ruler on the rug with a pillow over it and tugged at one end so that the ruler moved in and out from under the pillow. Oatmeal went bananas.

"You're just the sweetest little kitten in the whole wide world," I whispered, holding her close to my face, then cuddling her in my arms. She felt as though she had a motor inside her, the way her whole body vibrated when she purred.

I held her as I watched TV that night, and I suddenly realized that Lester hadn't asked to hold the kitten once. He hadn't petted her, either. It didn't seem possible that anyone could not like this kitten.

And then I remembered something from long ago. We had a dog once. It was Lester's dog. I think Uncle Milt gave it to him right after Mom died. It was a little dog with pointy ears named Tippy, and I remember Lester playing with it. I didn't. I was afraid of dogs then, the way they jump up on you and try to lick your face.

The longer I sat there with Oatmeal on my lap, the more I seemed to remember about Lester and Tippy. It was like trying to grab hold of a memory that was slipping over the edge of my mind. Now I had it and now I didn't. But I'm sure I remembered Lester lying on the rug and laughing, his arms up around his head, while Tippy tried to pry his arms away and lick his face. I remembered Lester and Tippy asleep in the same bed together. Tippy riding in the car with us.

Then I remembered something else. I *did* remember. The awful day that Lester was coming home from school, and somehow Tippy got out and saw Lester across the street. Tippy ran, and a car was coming, and . . .

I sucked in my breath and whimpered, only nobody heard it above the TV. I remembered Lester coming in the house screaming and Dad telling me to stay inside. And then somebody carried a little rolled-up rug over to Dad's car, and Dad put it in the trunk. Lester cried and cried, and we never had another dog after that. He didn't want one.

I knew someone who would have liked my kitten, though. I took Oatmeal upstairs and showed her my mother's picture. "You'd like her too, Oatmeal," I said. And my mama went right on smiling.

• • •

Donald Sheavers came over on Saturday to see Oatmeal. He liked her too. He showed me how to dangle
a string above her head, and Oatmeal would jump up
in the air and bat at it with her paw. He said we could
teach her the high jump.

But when he wanted to take her next door and intro-
duce her to Killer, I said no. I didn't want his dog anywhere near my kitten, even if you called him "Muffin."

"They'd go good together," Donald said. "Muffin and
Oatmeal."

Sometimes I think Donald Sheavers was dropped on
his head as a baby.

Mrs. Sheavers heard we had a cat and came over to
see it too. "Isn't that just the sweetest little thing?" she
said, and rubbed noses with the kitten. She asked me
where my dad was, and I told her he was at work at
the music store.

"He's a musician?" she asked.

"Yes," I said.

"I play the ukulele," she said.

Then I didn't worry about Mrs. Sheavers anymore. I
didn't think my dad would fall in love with a woman
who played the ukulele.

It was Lester who should have got a present, though,
because his sixteenth birthday was on Sunday.

"Les, we've been so busy getting moved in that your birthday just sneaked up on me," Dad said. "How would you like to celebrate? What would you like for a present?"

Lester was stretched out on the couch looking at a *Sports Illustrated* magazine. It was full of pictures of women in bathing suits. "I'd settle for this little number in the red bikini," he said.

Dad gave him a look.

"You could also get me a sports car. Actually, any Mercedes will do," said Lester.

"Something within reason, Les," Dad said.

"The best present you could possibly give me is to take me to get my learner's permit," said Lester. "You said I could drive when we got to Maryland."

"It's a deal," said Dad. "I'll take off early on Monday and we'll go. How's that?"

"Great!" said Lester.

I realized I'd been so busy with my kitten that I hadn't thought much about Lester's birthday either. A sixteenth birthday is a biggie! I looked around the house to see what I could give him for a present. Last year he gave me a cactus for my birthday. I supposed I could tie a bow around it and give it back, but somehow that didn't seem right.

Then I got this great idea. When Lester went down in the basement later to play his drums, I found the picture of the girl in the red bikini in his magazine. She was sitting sideways on the edge of a pool with her knees bent and her face up toward the sun. I took my scissors and carefully cut her out.

Then I went through an envelope of pictures that Aunt Sally had sent us. I found a photo my cousin Carol had taken of Lester at the going-away party they gave for us. Lester was sitting on the couch grinning, with a Coke in one hand and a hot dog in the other. I cut away the top of the photograph, carefully cutting out the hot dog and the Coke so that the only thing left was Lester on the couch.

I pasted him on a sheet of white cardboard that comes in Dad's shirts from the laundry. Then I pasted the girl in the red bikini on Lester's lap in the photo. It looked like one of his hands was under her knees and the other behind her head. Her body was a little bigger than his in the picture, but it didn't matter. It still looked like Lester with a girl on his lap.

Next I went back in my room and looked through the boxes of stuff I still hadn't unpacked. I found a bag of Little Princess cosmetics that Carol had given me once, with a mirror, a comb, and raspberry-flavored lip gloss in it. I smeared the lip gloss all over my lips.

Then I pressed my lips to the cardboard beside Lester's picture and made a lipstick kiss. The magazine said that the model's name was Angela, so I took a pen and wrote beside the lipstick kiss, *To Lester, from Angela, love and kisses.*

On Sunday Lester got to have whatever he wanted for dinner, so Dad brought home an order of Buffalo wings, a giant-sized sausage-and-onion pizza, and a chocolate mousse cake. We ate it around our big coffee table, the one we got from Goodwill, in the living room. Dad gave Lester a gift certificate from the Melody Inn so he could buy a bunch of cassettes.

Then I handed Lester a large yellow envelope I'd found in the wastebasket. He reached in and pulled out the cardboard with his picture on it. He stared at it, and then he threw back his head and laughed. He showed it to Dad, and Dad laughed too.

"Good present, Al!" Lester said. "I'll show it to the guys. And when I get my driver's license, you get one free trip wherever you want to go."

"Niagara Falls?" I said.

"Well, maybe not *that* far," said Lester.

The phone rang just then and I answered. It was a girl calling Lester to wish him a happy birthday.

The phone rang again later, and this time it was a different girl.

I looked at Dad. "Do you think he's forgotten Amy Miller?" I asked.

"I think we could say that," said Dad.

• • •

At school on Monday, I was standing in line at the drinking fountain with the Terrible Triplets. Once I started thinking of them as the Terrible Triplets, it was hard to stop.

"I got a kitten last Friday," I said.

Megan and Dawn and Jody just looked at me. Finally Megan said, "What's its name?"

"Oatmeal," I said.

"Oatmeal?" they cried together, and laughed.

"What kind of a name is that?" said Jody.

"She's the color of oatmeal and cream," I told them.

"I hate oatmeal," said Dawn.

"Me too," said Jody.

But I was feeling too good about my kitten to let the Triplets upset me. At recess, when Mrs. Burstin was patrolling the playground, she stopped to talk. "How are you liking Takoma Park, Alice?" she said. "It's certainly different from Chicago, isn't it?"

I nodded. "I have a kitten," I said. "My dad gave it to me last Friday."

"How wonderful!" she said. "Male or female?"

"Female."

"What color?"

"The color of oatmeal. And that's her name."

She laughed. "That's a nice name for a kitten." Then

she said, "You must have a pretty nice dad. He knows when a girl needs a friend."

I sort of wished she hadn't said that because this meant it showed. That everyone seemed to know everyone else on the playground except me. And that my father, guessing how I felt, had bought me a kitten to take the place of a friend.

Oh, well, I thought. *I've got Dad and Lester and Donald and Oatmeal. It's a start.*

❀ ❀ 5 ❀ ❀

Riding with Lester

When I got home from school on Monday, I found that Dad had taken Lester out of school over the lunch hour to get his learner's permit, and they were getting ready now for their first driving lesson.

"But here's the deal," Dad said. "And, Alice, the same goes for you when you get to be sixteen. Once you actually get your license, you can't have anyone in the car with you except family for the first six months. After that, if you don't get a ticket or have an accident during that time—even a fender bender—then you can have a friend or two along. But not until then."

"Daaaad!" Lester howled. But Dad was firm.

"What about you, Alice?" Dad said, looking at me. "Do you want to go over to the Sheaverses' while we're out, or do you want to come along for Lester's driving lesson?"

I was playing with Oatmeal and had to think about it a minute. If Lester was going to wreck the car, did I want to die along with my family or be left behind as an orphan?

"I guess I'll go," I said. "But be careful, Lester. I'm just a little girl with my whole life ahead of me."

"Hey, I want to live too," Lester said. "And I already know the basics. It's not like I can't steer or anything."

Dad just grunted. "Les, get the broom and mop, and Alice, bring up the two metal buckets from the basement."

Sometimes Dad doesn't make any sense at all. Lester was going to drive the car, not wash it. But we put all the stuff in the trunk, and Dad drove to the parking lot of a large restaurant that was closed on Mondays. He got out and came around on the passenger side, and Lester climbed over into the driver's seat. I sat up on my knees in the backseat so that when Lester crashed into something, I could see it coming.

"Sit down, Al. Your head's blocking the rear window," Lester said.

I sat down and fastened my seat belt.

"Okay," said Dad. "Start the engine, press the clutch pedal down, and practice shifting through all the gears."

Lester started the car. I could hear his big sneakers squeaking against each other as they took their places on the pedals.

"Dad, when are we going to get an automatic?" he grumbled.

"When we get a new car, which won't be for a while now, so stop complaining," Dad said. "Now ease the clutch out in first gear and practice going forward, then reverse."

Lester's shoes clumped and squeaked again, and the Honda shot forward.

"Wheeee!" I cried.

"Easy on the gas," said Dad.

Lester braked and this time *we* shot forward.

"Not so hard on the brake," said Dad.

It didn't take long for Lester to get the hang of just how hard to press the pedals, and he practiced driving around the empty lot, making turns and backing up.

"Okay. Let's do some parallel parking," said Dad. "Stop the car."

He got out, opened the trunk, and put the buckets about twenty feet apart, six feet out from the curb in front of the restaurant. Then he set the broom in one, the mop in the other. This time I got out because I wanted to watch Lester try to park between the buckets.

"Okay, Les," Dad said, getting back in the car. "Pull up past the first bucket, then back into the space between them."

I watched the car jerk forward. Lester forgot to put it

in reverse. Then the car stopped and slowly started to move backward. But it swung in too far and the tires bumped the curb. I waved my arms dramatically and pretended I'd been hit.

Lester rolled down his window. "Cut it out, Alice!" he said. He pulled the car forward again and tried to park between the buckets. This time he knocked over the broom. I cheered.

"Alice," said Dad, getting out to set the broom back up again, "be a helper, not a hindrance."

I didn't know what a hindrance was, but I'll bet it wasn't good. So I took off my jacket and hung it on the broom handle so Lester could see it better.

He tried again. This time he carefully maneuvered past the broom, but he hit the mop. I tried to keep a straight face as I set the mop up again.

"Shut up," Lester said to me, even though I hadn't said a word.

He tried again, and still again, but he never did a very good job of parking. "It's not like real parking, Dad," he said. "I need real cars to practice on."

"Not yet, you don't," said Dad.

"Well, at least let me drive around the neighborhood," Lester begged.

"I suppose you can handle that," said Dad.

I helped put the buckets and stuff back in the trunk and climbed in the backseat again. "Don't hit any little children, Lester." I laughed. I thought how funny it would be if I had a lipstick and wrote outside the car window, *Help! I'm being kidnapped!* Maybe a police car would see it and pull Lester over. Or if I had a paper sack and blew it up and popped it, and Lester would think he'd blown a tire.

Lester drove slowly up and down the streets of our neighborhood and was doing just fine until he came to a stoplight at the top of a hill. It turned red just as we reached it, and Lester put on the brake.

"Oh, boy," I heard Dad breathe out. "Now, this might be a little tricky, Les."

It was. When the light turned green and Lester took his foot off the brake, the car started rolling backward. I screamed.

"Alice, will you *stop!*" Lester yelled, slamming on the brakes, and we all jerked forward.

"You've got to let out the clutch about the same time you're taking your foot off the brake and giving it gas," Dad told him. "It takes practice, Les. Just go slow and easy."

But when Lester took his foot off the brake a second time, the car rolled backward again. The car behind us honked, and Lester slammed on the brakes a second time. I put my head down on the seat so he couldn't see I was laughing.

"Try it again, Lester," Dad said calmly. "Take your left

foot off the clutch and your right foot off the brake and try to do it together. Give it gas before it starts to roll."

This time the car shot forward, but the light changed and we had to stop all over again, sticking out into the intersection so that cars had to swerve around us.

"Dad, why don't we get a car with power brakes and power steering?" Lester cried.

"Because it's good for you to know how to drive all kinds of cars," Dad said. "Don't get rattled, now. Everyone was a beginner once."

"Even you?" I asked. "Who taught you to drive, Dad?"

"Charlie, my favorite brother. He is a lot older than me and made a good teacher."

We waited for the light to turn green again. Now there were three other cars backed up behind us, not just one.

The light turned green, and Lester was so anxious to make it that he moved his feet too fast and killed the engine. The car behind us made a U-turn and went tearing off in the opposite direction. So did the car behind it.

"Easy does it, Lester," Dad said.

I wanted to laugh, but then I remembered how long it had taken me to learn to ride a two-wheeler. I think it was Uncle Milt who bought a bike for me after Mother died, and it was Lester who ran along beside me while I rode to help me keep my balance. It was Lester who taught me to whistle, too, and to blow bubble gum. Who made me my first pair of tin-can stilts.

I sat up very straight in the backseat so Lester could see that I wasn't laughing at him. The next time the light turned green, Lester pulled out into the intersection and made it through, a little jerkily, but at least no one honked.

"Good job, Lester," I said.

We stayed out for another half hour, and Lester did everything right. He pulled in the driveway when we got home as smoothly as a train coming into a station.

"You're going to be a great driver, Lester, and I'll go with you anywhere," I said. "Even Niagara Falls."

"Very good, indeed!" said Dad.

Lester was practically crowing when he got out and went right to the phone to call his friends.

Dad was in a good mood too, so I thought maybe it was the right time to ask for something for myself.

"Next week, can we get my ears pierced?" I asked.

Dad lowered his newspaper and stared at me over the business page. "Don't even think it," he said.

6

Call from Chicago

Lester didn't seem to have any trouble making friends. Not only did two girls call him on his birthday, but we had only been in Maryland a few weeks before he had a little combo to play in. Every Sunday three other boys came to our house to play music down in the basement.

Lester played the drums, of course. Two of the boys brought their electric guitars, and the third one played the cornet. Dad called them the "Explosive Four." The boys called their combo "The Naked Nomads" because it was so warm in our basement that they took off their shirts when they played. And as soon as the music started, Dad always said the same thing: "Saints preserve us!" The house shook, and Oatmeal hid behind the couch.

"Why do you call yourselves nomads?" I asked Lester once.

"Because we'll go wherever someone wants us to play," said Lester.

"Who's asked you to play?" I said.

"No one," said Lester.

The thing is, they could only practice when Dad was home. We're not allowed to have friends in when he's not here. And Lester had to come right home from school to be here for me. "That may be a problem later on," Dad said, "but right now I'm doing the best I can."

One Sunday they were practicing in the basement when we got a call from Aunt Sally. The music was so loud that the only way I could hear her was to drag the phone into the coat closet and close the door after me. I leaned against our boot box and cradled the phone against my ear.

"What's all that noise in the background?" asked Aunt Sally.

"Music," I told her.

"Alice, your father never listened to that kind of music before," she said.

"He doesn't have any choice," I said. "Lester has some friends here."

"Oh?" I couldn't tell if she was pleased or worried. "Lester's made some friends?"

"He makes friends in a hurry," I said. "He has three of them right now, and they're all down in the basement."

"The basement?" I could tell now it was worry.

"They've got a combo going," I told her. "And Lester's playing the drums. It's sort of loud."

"I can hear that. Who are these boys, Alice?"

"I don't know. Some guys from school, I think. I don't know their real names, but Lester calls them 'Billy' and 'Psycho' and 'Ape.'"

There was silence at the end of the line, and I wondered if Aunt Sally was still there.

"Is your father down there with them?" she asked. "I mean, they *do* have adult supervision, don't they?"

"No, Dad's working on a crossword puzzle," I said. "He doesn't go down there unless he has to."

"Is this a bona fide group, Alice? Does it have a name?"

"The Naked Nomads," I told her.

"What?"

"Because they take off some of their clothes and—"

"Alice, put your father on right away," she said.

Ten minutes later, when Dad came out of the closet, he said, "Alice, the next time your Aunt Sally calls, God bless her, I am fine, you are fine, Lester is fine, the cat is fine, we are all fine and eating our vegetables, and we haven't burned the house down yet. Okay?"

I grinned. "Okay," I told him.

• • •

The next day at school, we had art class. We had to choose partners, and the Terrible Triplets were upset because one of them would have to find someone else to be partners with. They asked the art teacher if the three of them could do their project together, and she said no, we had to be in pairs.

I proved I could be just as stuck-up as they could by looking the other way when Jody turned in my direction. When a chubby girl asked if I wanted to be her partner, I said, "Sure."

We were studying mirror images, and each pair was given a large sheet of paper folded down the middle, from top to bottom. We could use any colors we wanted and draw any design we wanted, but everything that one person drew on one side of the fold had to be copied by the other person exactly the same way on the other side, but in the opposite direction.

"Think of a heart," the teacher said, and drew a large valentine heart on the blackboard. Then she drew a line down the middle of it and showed us that the two halves of the heart were exactly the same, only the lines on the left side were going one way and the lines on the right side were going the other.

My partner's name was Rosalind, and I'd never paid much attention to her before. In the art room, where we shared a table, she said, "My brother plays in a combo with your brother."

I looked at her. "He does? The Naked Nomads?"

She giggled and suddenly we both started laughing. Just the name made us laugh.

"When the two girls at the second table stop laughing, we can begin," the art teacher said.

Rosalind and I wiped the smiles off our faces, but we were still smiling on the inside. Every time our eyes met, we tried to keep our mouths straight, and that made us giggle. Once we started planning our design, we were friends. Just like that. Because of the giggles.

Our design was pretty ordinary. We drew a heart just like the one on the blackboard, but then we added a lot of twists and curls, and whatever one girl did on her side of the paper, the other one did on hers, drawing it backward. It wasn't as easy as it looked.

"Why don't you come over too, the next time your brother comes to our house?" I asked Rosalind.

"Maybe I will," she said.

When The Naked Nomads met at our house again, Rosalind came too. Her brother was one of the guitar players, Billy.

"I brought the brat," Billy said to my brother when they came in. "I guess our sisters are friends."

"Okay by me," said Lester.

I could tell that Dad was really, really happy about it. He said that Rosalind could come over whenever she wanted. He let us have the TV; he made some popcorn for us; and he even made hot-fudge sundaes, he was so glad I had a friend.

Rosalind lives about six blocks away up the hill. Megan, one of the Terrible Triplets, lives only two blocks away in the other direction. I wished it was Rosalind who lived only two blocks away and Megan who lived up the hill. Rosalind and I are a lot alike because we laugh at the same things. She has two brothers instead of one, though, and a stepmom, too.

At school we started doing things together. We always ate at the same table at lunch, and in gym, when we had to pair up again for square dancing and the Terrible Triplets had one too many, Megan and Jody paired up and Dawn had to find someone else. She asked me if I'd be her partner, and I got to say, "Sorry, I'm with Rosalind." That felt as sweet as sugar coming out of my mouth.

You never know what's going to come out of Rosalind's mouth, though. We were talking once about whether or not there would be snow for Christmas, and Rosalind said she didn't think so. She said the earth is getting warmer, and a hundred years from now, Takoma Park will be a lake. She said if we came back to Maryland then, we'd all be riding around in boats. I never know whether to believe her or not.

But she knows a lot about animals. At lunch one day,

a girl at our table brought in a snake's skin and said it was a poisonous water moccasin's. Rosalind said no, it wasn't, it was from a common water snake. When Dawn asked how she knew so much about animals, Rosalind said she wants to work at the National Zoo when she grows up. "Where? In the elephant house?" Dawn said, and everyone laughed. But afterward, Rosalind told me that's exactly where she *does* want to work: with elephants.

One reason she likes to come to our house, though, is to play with Oatmeal. Her father's allergic to cats and dogs, so she has only goldfish and a turtle. What she would really like, I guess, is an elephant, but you don't exactly see many of those in Maryland.

The reason *I* like Rosalind to come over is because, number one, she likes to play with Oatmeal; number two, she laughs a lot; and number three, if she doesn't know the answer to something, she just makes it up. I can't exactly trust her, but at least she's interesting.

7

Sweethearts

Donald Sheavers never has any idea what he wants to do when he comes over. He'll do anything I ask. If I say, "Let's play Monopoly, Donald," he'll play Monopoly. If I say, "Let's make hot chocolate," he'll say, "Okay." If I say, "What do you want to do, Donald?" he'll say, "I don't know; what do you want to do?" I'll bet if I ever said, "Put your shoes on your ears, Donald," his sneakers would be on both sides of his head.

Dad wouldn't let me go out on Halloween by myself, so I said, "Want to go trick-or-treating, Donald?"

"Okay," he said. I figured I was getting old enough to go trick-or-treating without Dad or Lester along now.

"What are you going to be?" I asked.

"I don't know," said Donald.

"You want to go as a ghost?" I said, thinking of the most stupid, common thing that came to mind.

"Okay," said Donald.

"*No*, Donald! Think of something really different!" I said.

"Okay," said Donald.

I waited a minute or two. "Have you thought of something?" I asked.

"No," said Donald.

"Why don't you be a werewolf?" I said.

"Okay," said Donald.

"Do you know what a werewolf looks like?"

"No."

Donald is hopeless.

"Donald, be something that you *know*. A vampire, even."

"Okay," said Donald.

On Halloween night Donald came over to get me. He had an old sheet over his head, with two holes cut in it for his eyes. There were huge fangs coming out of the slit where his mouth should be, and his hands had two big werewolf paws on them. Nobody knew what he was, but he looked fabulous.

I was a gypsy girl. For the Halloween party at school, I'd been Schubert. Every year Dad lets me wear the jacket of his old tuxedo and I dress up as a composer, carrying a baton. It's quick and easy! But I wanted to be something else when we went out for tricks or treats, so I was a gypsy. I wasn't fabulous. I looked ordinary.

"Gracious!" people said when we knocked on their doors. They all looked at Donald. "What are *you* supposed to be?"

Nobody asked me because they already knew what a gypsy girl was. Donald couldn't answer because of the fangs, but he looked so great, we got caramel apples, super-size Milky Way bars, bags of candy corn, quarters, and soft-dough pretzels.

When we were crossing the street at the corner, we passed a cowgirl and her horse. Well, it was a girl wearing a horse's head. The other girl was holding the reins and laughing at the way her horse kicked and bucked. I recognized the laugh.

"Rosalind?" I said.

"Alice?" said Rosalind.

Donald couldn't speak because of his fangs, so I had to tell her who he was. Rosalind was out trick-or-treating with her cousin Tracy, who lives in D.C.

"Say hi, Tracy," Rosalind said.

Her horse only neighed and bucked again. They'd collected even more stuff than we had.

"You want to come back to my house for some pop or something?" I asked.

"Some *what?*" said Tracy.

"Pop."

"She means soda," said Rosalind.

I didn't know that out East it's called soda. In Chicago it was always pop.

"Okay," said Tracy. So we all went back to my house. Lester was eating popcorn in the living room, so we poured out our candy on the kitchen table. I traded my Baby Ruth bars and Butterfingers for Milk Duds and jelly beans. Then I opened a big bottle of Pepsi and poured some into four cups. Tracy drank the most. She had short blond hair and dark brown eyes that looked like coat buttons.

When the Pepsi was gone, Tracy asked, "What are you going to do with the bottle?"

"I don't know," I said. "Do you want it?"

"We could play spin the bottle," she said.

I couldn't believe she was serious. Tracy looked at Donald. "You want to play spin the bottle, Donald?"

"Okay," said Donald.

"Oh, no!" I said. "I'm not playing spin the bottle. I'm not kissing Donald."

"This is a fortune-telling game, it's not kissing," said Tracy. "Just think of a question and the bottle will tell you the answer."

"Okay," I said. We all sat down on the floor in a sort of circle with the bottle in the middle.

"Which one of us will be the richest?" asked Donald.

Tracy picked up the Pepsi bottle and held it mysteriously out in front of her. Then she slowly brought it close to her face and blew down inside it, making a ghostly whistle. "Whoooo," she said into the bottle, "will be the richest one here?"

She put the bottle back on the floor and spun it around, and when it stopped, it was pointing at Tracy.

"Oh, I'm the lucky one!" Tracy cried happily. "What else do you want to know?"

We thought for a moment. "Who will be the most famous?" I asked.

Tracy brought the bottle to her lips again and blew down inside it. "Whooooo," she said, "will be the most famous one here?"

Again she spun the bottle, and—guess what?—the bottle pointed to Tracy.

"Hey! You stopped it with your finger," said Donald. "I'll spin it next time."

"Okay, I've got a question," said Rosalind. "Which one of us is going to be kissed?"

Donald spun the bottle around and it pointed to me. I jumped to my feet. "Not me!" I said. "I'm not kissing anyone."

"Let's try this one," said Rosalind. "Who is going to die first?" This time she spun the bottle as hard as she could, and we all jumped up, stumbling over our feet, to get out of the room before the bottle stopped spinning. Lester was coming into the kitchen just then with a half-empty bowl of popcorn, and Tracy ran right into him. There was popcorn all over the place—the floors, the chairs, Tracy, Lester.

"Hey, let's spin the bottle and see who goes home first," said Lester.

"I'm sorry," said Tracy.

We all got down on our hands and knees and started picking up popcorn. I caught Rosalind's eye and could tell she was trying not to laugh. So was I.

Just then Oatmeal woke up and came out into the kitchen. She saw the popcorn and started batting it around the floor, chasing it under the table and through the legs of chairs. This got us all laughing, even Lester.

When Halloween was over, I said, "Lester, did you ever play spin the bottle?"

"My favorite game," he said.

"Did you kiss?"

"Sure."

"Who?"

"Some girl named Gloria Kingsberry."

"Was she your girlfriend?"

"No," said Lester.

"Did you like her?"

"Not particularly," Lester told me.

"Why did you like kissing her, then?"

"Because she'd just eaten a doughnut and had powdered sugar all around the rim of her mouth," he said.

"That's gross," I told him.

"Not as gross as kissing Caroline Mullins."

"What was wrong with Caroline?"

"She had a runny nose," said Lester.

Don't ever talk to Lester on Halloween, or you won't want to eat any more of your candy.

At school on Monday, Rosalind told me that Tracy wants Donald to be her boyfriend. I didn't like hearing that. I didn't particularly want Donald Sheavers to be *my* boyfriend. I just didn't want him to be Tracy's.

At lunchtime Rosalind asked Donald if he wanted to be Tracy's boyfriend.

"I don't know," he said.

Rosalind giggled. "Do you want to be *my* boyfriend?"

"I don't know," said Donald.

"Do you want to be Alice's boyfriend?" asked Rosalind.

Donald looked at me. "Okay," he said.

I could feel my face growing hot.

The Triplets had heard what Rosalind said to Donald.

"Hey, everybody!" yelled Megan. "Donald is Alice's

boyfriend!" And the Terrible Triplets began to chant:

> "Donald and Al-ice,
> Sitting in a tree,
> K-I-S-S-I-N-G!"

And then the whole table began to call out, "Kiss her, Donald! Kiss her!"

"Okay," said Donald, grinning. He got up from his chair at the next table and came around to ours. I slid under the table. Everyone peeked under to watch. All I could see were feet and faces. All the feet came forward and tried to trap me so Donald could catch me. Everyone was screaming and laughing.

The principal came into the lunchroom.

"Children?" he called.

They went on screaming. He clapped his hands for attention.

The screaming stopped.

"What's going on?" Mr. Serio asked.

"Donald's kissing Alice," somebody said.

Mrs. Burstin hurried across the room. "Donald, sit down," she said. "Where's Alice?"

"Under the table," everyone cried.

All the feet stopped swinging. I saw Mrs. Burstin's legs. Then I saw her face looking at me under the table.

"Come out of there, Alice," she said.

Now my face was so hot, it felt as though it was on fire. I crawled out from under the table. "You shouldn't be under the table at lunchtime," she said. "Are you through eating?"

I wasn't. I'd hardly even started, but I nodded yes.

"Then take care of your lunch bag and go outside," she said.

I could feel my cheeks burning. I took my lunch bag with my half-eaten sandwich in it and dropped it in the trash. My Hostess cupcake went with it.

Rosalind raised her hand. "I'm through too," she said.

"Then you may go outside also," said Mrs. Burstin.

Donald raised his hand.

"No," said the teacher. "You stay in here."

Out on the playground, Rosalind said, "I'm sorry. I didn't mean to get you in trouble."

"I know," I said.

"Megan and her big mouth," said Rosalind.

"Yeah," I said.

"Are you mad at me?" asked Rosalind.

"A little," I told her.

"Is there anything I can do?" she asked.

"Tell Tracy to go jump in the lake," I answered.

8

Embarrassing Moments

I think that more embarrassing things happen to me than to anyone else. My very first memory is an embarrassing moment. Lester says he can remember being in his crib. He says that Mama and Dad were giving a party and guests came in his bedroom and looked down at him. He says he can still remember the wallpaper.

The very first thing I remember is a day in nursery school. I had to go the bathroom, but I couldn't get the door open. I don't know why I didn't ask the teacher to open it for me. I just went back and sat in my little chair and wet myself and wet the chair, and when someone said, "This chair is wet!" I said I'd spilled some lemonade. We didn't even have lemonade.

And I remember playing in Aunt Sally's flower garden

even after she'd told me not to. When I saw her coming out of the house, I knew I couldn't run away in time, so I just lay down in the dirt and pretended I was dead.

Then there was the time Uncle Milt took Carol and Lester and me to the movies and I got the hiccups and hiccuped all through the movie, and finally the people in front of us got up and sat somewhere else.

Sometimes I wish that after I do something stupid, my face would change and no one who saw me do it would ever recognize me again.

I remember thinking once, when I was in kindergarten and cried during a thunderstorm, that maybe once I got to first grade I wouldn't do things like that anymore. When I got to first grade and was still doing embarrassing things, I told myself that maybe when I got to second grade my life would be different, but it wasn't. I mashed my teacher's fingers in the door. And now that I was in third grade, I decided that nothing was going to change there, either.

"Did you ever do anything embarrassing?" I asked Lester one morning at the table.

"Huh-uh. I'm perfect," said Lester, and poured half the syrup over the pancakes on his plate.

"You never wet your pants?" I asked.

"Hey, Al, I'm eating breakfast," he said.

"Embarrassing things go on happening to people all

their lives," Dad said. "It's part of being alive."

I didn't want to hear about it.

"They're just different kinds of things," said Dad.

"Like what?" I asked.

"Like forgetting people's names. Like thinking Mr. Brown is Mr. Green and going up and saying, 'Hi, Ted, how are you?'"

Somehow that didn't seem as embarrassing as mashing your teacher's fingers.

"I was playing musical chairs at a party once, and when the music stopped, I sat on a girl's lap," Lester said.

That didn't seem as embarrassing, either.

"Okay, here's one," said Lester. "When I was in seventh grade, I had just put a problem on the blackboard and found out my pants were unzipped."

"That's pretty embarrassing," I agreed.

"Not only that," said Lester, "but when someone told me about it and I tried to pull the zipper up, it got caught in my undershorts and I had to go to the nurse and have her help me get loose."

"Oh, that *is* embarrassing!" I said.

"But he's still here to tell about it," said Dad. "You don't die from embarrassment."

"*Everybody* does embarrassing things sometimes, Alice," Lester told me. "The most powerful person you can ever imagine has done things he doesn't want anyone to know about. Even the president of the United States."

When I went to school the next day, I looked around the classroom and thought about it. That meant that everyone there, including the Terrible Triplets—the *teacher,* even—had embarrassing things happen to them.

I decided to test Rosalind on it.

"What is the most embarrassing thing that ever happened to you?" I asked.

I was surprised to see her face turn pink. "I'm not going to tell," she said.

That was all I needed to know.

One Saturday, Dad asked if I wanted to spend the afternoon at the Melody Inn. I had seen the music store only once, when we first moved here from Chicago. Dad had taken Lester and me in on a Sunday to show us the place, but I'd never visited the store when it was open.

He said he would come home at noon and pick me up, take me to lunch, and then I could spend the afternoon with him. I put on my blue tights and a blue-and-green dress and brushed my hair. Dad took me to a sub shop, where we shared a Caesar sub with everything on it—meat and cheese and black olives and tomatoes.

"Is this where you always eat lunch?" I asked Dad.

"Sometimes. Or sometimes Janice brings me a sandwich."

"Is she the one who gave us the kitten?" I asked.

"Yes. She's in charge of the sheet music department," said Dad.

I felt very grown-up, going to my Dad's store, and everyone smiled at me. I guess when you're the boss's daughter, they have to smile and act nice. I smiled back and pretended I knew what they were talking about when they showed me the brass instruments and the woodwind section and the string alcove.

There are two floors to the Melody Inn. On the first floor, right in the middle, is a grand piano, with smaller pianos around it. There are violins along one wall, horns along another. And trays and bins filled with all sorts of stuff like guitar picks and strings and instrument oil. The other side of the store has cassettes and sheet music.

The second floor is divided into little soundproof cubicles where instructors give music lessons to students.

But the place I like best is the Gift Shoppe under the stairs. The sign says, EVERYTHING YOU WANT FOR THE MUSIC-MINDED. There are fun presents. Little plaster busts of Mozart and Bach. Scarves with a piano keyboard printed on them. Pads of paper with CHOPIN-

LISZT (shopping list) at the top. Chopin and Liszt are composers, see. Dad had to explain that one to me.

There are coffee mugs with signatures of singers on them and perfume bottles shaped like violins. But best of all is the gift wheel. It's a lighted display case with a button to press, which makes the whole case go around so you can see shelf after shelf of jewelry.

There are pins in the shape of French horns. Earrings that look like clef signs. There are books about Strauss and vases with photos of concert halls on them. Music boxes that play Brahms's *Lullaby* and necklaces that dangle little silver C notes from a chain. If you see something you like, you press the button again and the wheel stops turning. Then a clerk can reach in and get it for you.

I remembered to pronounce Mozart "Mote-Zart," with a "t," and to firmly shake Janice Sherman's hand when Dad introduced me to her. Lester says the worst thing you can do when you meet someone is to give them the "dead-fish" handshake, meaning your hand goes limp and the other person has to do all the work.

"Janice, this is my daughter, Alice," Dad said.

I gave her a nice firm handshake and smiled my brightest smile.

Janice Sherman is a medium-sized woman with brown hair and brown eyes. She was wearing a gray wool dress and her glasses on a chain around her neck.

She looked very orderly to me. I'll bet if you went to Janice Sherman's house, all her underwear would be arranged in her drawers in alphabetical order.

The strange thing about Janice was the way she kept flicking her teeth with her tongue while she talked. I was glad when we left Janice and Dad introduced me to the clerk in the Gift Shoppe and the instructor who taught trombone.

But Saturday is the busiest day at the Melody Inn, so Dad told me I would have to entertain myself while he waited on customers. Loretta Jenkins, the girl who clerks and runs the Gift Shoppe on Saturdays, let me help her unpack a carton of music boxes with little brass horns glued to the tops. They played "Seventy-Six Trombones" when you wound them up.

All the iced tea I had drunk for lunch made me need the bathroom, though, and Loretta showed me where to go. When I was washing my hands afterward, I looked in the mirror and then I froze because I seemed to have a tooth missing! I couldn't believe it! There was a big dark hole beneath my upper gum! I ran my tongue quickly over my teeth to feel the empty place, and a piece of black olive slid off my tooth.

Then I knew why Janice Sherman had been moving her tongue. I thought of all the people I had smiled at since I'd come in the store. I couldn't stand it!

I went back out to Loretta, who wore her frizzy hair in a huge sunburst around her head, and smiled my widest possible smile, but she wasn't even looking at me. She was dusting the music boxes.

I felt I had to go around the whole store and smile at everyone I'd smiled at before so they could see I had all my teeth. I went upstairs to the second floor and looked in all the glass cubicles until I came to the trombone instructor. He was giving a lesson with his back to me. I stood there grinning with my lips apart, while the boy he was teaching stared back at me. When the instructor turned around to see what the boy was looking at, I smiled a bigger smile than ever. The instructor reached up and pulled a curtain.

I went back down and wandered all around the store, grinning at everyone in sight. Then I went back to Janice Sherman, who was writing up a customer's order, and smiled broadly. She looked at me and then at the customer. "Mrs. Levine, this is Mr. McKinley's daughter," she said.

"How do you do?" I said, and put out my hand. The woman took it, and I made sure it wasn't a dead-fish handshake.

That done, I went back to help Loretta unpack the rest of the stuff for the Gift Shoppe. When I sat down on the little stool behind the counter to open the next box, I saw a long piece of toilet paper stuck to the bottom of my shoe.

Oh no! First I'd gone around the whole store with a black olive over one tooth, and then I'd walked around trailing toilet paper.

I put my head in my lap and wished I could keep it there forever.

"Are you sick?" asked Loretta.

"I'm sick of myself," I said, and told her about the black olive and the toilet paper. "Is there ever a time you stop doing dumb things?" I asked her.

"Yes," she said.

"When I'm forty? Fifty?" I asked.

"When you're dead," said Loretta.

I just wished I could erase the last two months and start all over again. I wished that when Megan, Dawn, and Jody danced along the sidewalk in front of me on the first day of school, I'd said something nice to them instead of pretending to tie my shoe. Then we could have been quadruplets together. I wished I'd smiled at all the other girls I didn't know in my class instead of waiting for people to come over and make friends with *me*. I wished that when Rosalind asked Donald if he wanted to be my boyfriend, I had said, "Well, *I* don't want him to be a boyfriend of *mine!*" instead of crawling under the table, and that when I had lunch with Dad, I'd ordered a grilled cheese sandwich instead of a sub with black olives. How do you ever make friends in a new place if you keep on doing stupid things all the time? If you don't have a mother to tell you what's what? If you don't even have your Aunt Sally?

❀ ❀ 9 ❀ ❀

Hello and Good-bye

I knew that Dad's favorite brother was getting married over Thanksgiving, but I didn't know we were going to Tennessee for Uncle Charlie's wedding.

"I'd rather eat toads," said Lester.

"You don't have a choice," said Dad.

"Do I *have* to?" Lester hollered. "I *hate* weddings! I *hate* dressing up. Why can't I stay here?"

"Because I would have to be brain-dead to leave a sixteen-year-old boy alone in a house over a holiday weekend, that's why," said Dad. "You either come with us, or spend Thanksgiving with your Aunt Sally in Chicago."

I didn't think that would be so bad at all, but at the very mention of Aunt Sally, Lester changed his mind. "Okay, I'll go," he grumbled, "but I won't enjoy it."

"You don't have to enjoy it," said Dad. "You just have to show your support for a fifty-seven-year-old man who finally decided to get married."

"What took him so long?" I asked.

"I guess he was just looking for the right woman, and Marge happened to be the one," said Dad.

Suddenly I didn't want to go. "Who will take care of Oatmeal?" I cried. "I can't go off and leave her."

"I've already asked Mrs. Sheavers to look after her," Dad said. "And you know, this will be a good chance to see Grandpa McKinley too, because he's ninety-three now, and may not be around much longer."

We're sort of short on relatives. My mother's parents died in a car crash when she was away at college, and Grandma McKinley died of a heart attack before I was born. So that just left Mom's sister, Sally, in Chicago, and Dad's three brothers, Charlie and Harold and Howard, down in Tennessee, and a ninety-three-year-old grandfather, whom I hardly remembered. Except that for the last ten years he's been telling everyone he has only a few more months to live, Dad said.

"Hey, man, we're going to *party!*" Lester said sarcastically.

I always wished I'd had a nice fat grandmother with a big wide lap I could sit on. It didn't seem fair that I didn't have a mother or a grandmother, either. I'd just have to be satisfied with what relatives I had left, I told myself. So I went upstairs and began packing my bag for the wedding.

Mrs. Sheavers and Donald came over later to see about Oatmeal.

"Give her a scoop of this every morning and every evening," I said, showing them where we kept her food. "Here's her brush and here's her litter box. And she likes to be tickled under her chin."

"We'll take good care of the precious itty-bitty thing!" said Mrs. Sheavers. And she smiled so wide at Dad that I could see the molars at the back of her mouth.

"And keep her away from Killer," I added. Donald only grinned.

We got up at four on Thanksgiving morning and were on the road a half hour later. There must have been a zillion trucks on the highway but hardly any cars. I just curled up on the backseat with my pillow and went to sleep again. Lester sat up front with Dad, with headphones on his head, his eyes closed, listening to music.

The problem was, we kept having to stop to go to the bathroom, only none of us seemed to need a rest stop at the same time.

First we stopped for Lester, then we stopped for me, and when we stopped again for Lester, Dad said, "No more pop! No more orange juice, either, till we get to Tennessee. Alice, get out and go to the rest room too."

"I don't need to go," I said.

"I don't care. Get out and go anyway," said Dad. "Don't come back until you do."

I went inside the station and got the key to the ladies' room. I tore off some toilet paper and covered the seat. Then I sat down. Nothing happened. I *knew* nothing would happen. I sat on the toilet and watched a bug trying to crawl around the wastebasket. Then I counted the black-and-white tiles on the floor. I recited all the multiplication tables I'd learned so far, the Pledge of Allegiance, and a poem about clouds. I had just started in on "Ninety-nine Bottles of Beer on the Wall" when there was a tap on the door.

"It's occupied," I called out. That's what Aunt Sally always says when we're in a public rest room and somebody knocks. *It's occupied.*

"Alice?" came Lester's voice. "Dad says to hurry up."

"Sorry," I said. "He'll just have to wait."

"You'd better get out here!" he barked. "You're holding us up."

"Too bad," I said.

Three minutes went by, and there was another tap on the door.

"Al, get out here this minute," said Dad.

"Nothing's happened," I told him. "I told you it wouldn't."

"Then come out anyway. We've got to leave," he said.

As soon as he said that, I needed to use the toilet, and after that, Dad didn't complain anymore about bathroom stops, but he wouldn't let me drink anything, either.

We had our lunch at a truck stop. A big sign said, TURKEY AND ALL THE TRIMMINGS. There were a lot of truckers sitting on stools at the counter, their plates piled high with turkey and mashed potatoes and cranberry sauce. I was glad I wasn't a trucker having a Thanksgiving dinner in a diner.

Besides, the closer we got to Uncle Harold's, the more I wanted to see these relatives I didn't visit very often. Uncle Harold and Aunt Vivian didn't have any children—they said that taking care of Grandpa McKinley was all the children they could handle—and Uncle Howard and Aunt Linda's children were grown up. Of course, Uncle Charlie, who was just now getting married, didn't have any either. So Carol, Aunt Sally's daughter back in Chicago, was the only cousin I really knew.

"How come we're so short of relatives?" I asked Dad.

"Because that's the way the cookie crumbles," said Dad.

• • •

We got to Uncle Harold and Aunt Vivian's house about six in the evening, and everyone waited to have Thanksgiving dinner with us. I was passed around the room like a sack of sugar, everyone giving me a hug and everybody saying, "Look how she's grown!" so that I felt like Alice in Wonderland, where she grows so tall that she's a freak.

They didn't hug Lester, though; they just shook his hand and patted him on the shoulder. And I decided right then I was glad I was a girl. I would hate to go through life with dead-fish handshakes instead of nice warm hugs.

Somebody wheeled in Grandpa McKinley and put him at one end of the long table, with Lester and me at each side. Grandpa had shaggy eyebrows and dark brown eyes that rolled from me to Lester and back again.

"Who are you?" he demanded, staring hard at me, leaning forward to get a better look.

"A-Alice," I said. "Your granddaughter."

"Eh?" he said. "Eloise?"

Alice," I repeated, more loudly.

"Don't shout," he said, and turned to Lester. "Who's the noisy one?" he asked, nodding toward me.

"My sister," Lester told him. "I'm Lester. We're Ben's children."

"Oh," said Grandpa McKinley. He picked up his fork, then looked at Lester again. "Why aren't you in school?"

"Because it's Thanksgiving," said Lester, looking over at me, and we both tried hard not to laugh.

"Yes, happy Thanksgiving, Dad," our father said, coming over to Grandpa McKinley and giving him a kiss on the cheek.

"They came to see me get married," put in Uncle Charlie. "Remember what's happening this weekend?"

"You're getting married?" said Grandpa. "Now, who in tarnation would marry you?"

"I would," said Marge, my aunt-to-be, an apple-cheeked lady with heavy arms and a warm smile.

"Nobody tells me anything," Grandpa McKinley complained.

Somehow that put us all in a good mood, and chuckles traveled around the table and settled on Les and Grandpa and me. Grandpa liked cooked carrots. He ate every single one on his plate, then reached over with his fork and jabbed at mine when he thought I wasn't looking. When he finished mine, he went after Lester's, and everyone smiled some more. Everyone but Grandpa, who just chewed away under his scowl.

Dad's brothers talked with a southern flavor, which reminded me of the way Dad sounds sometimes when he's tired. They said "thank" instead of "think," "y'all" instead of "you all," and they left the "g" off the ends of words, so that I was "Alice darlin'." I decided I liked that just fine. I liked having relatives make a fuss over me and wanted to soak up every little bit of loving I could get.

On Friday everybody flew into action getting ready for Uncle Charlie's wedding the next day. No matter where I was sitting or standing, I felt I was in the way. And when Uncle Charlie asked if anybody wanted to ride with him to pick up his tuxedo, I said I'd go. I was afraid if I stuck around, I'd be put in charge of Grandpa, and I wasn't sure I could handle that.

We got in Uncle Charlie's Oldsmobile and headed downtown. He and Dad both looked a lot alike, same gray hair over their ears and they both had a twinkle in their eyes.

"You know," Uncle Charlie said, "it's a durn shame your dad and I live so far apart. Those twins are okay, but your dad was always special to me."

"What twins?" I asked.

"Harold and Howard."

"Oh," I said. I hadn't known they were twins. And then I said, "Dad says you taught him how to drive."

Uncle Charlie looked surprised. "Why, I'd forgotten all about that!" he said, and began to smile. "I don't suppose your dad told you about the time he drove the car to a shopping center and forgot where he'd parked it? Ben came out the wrong entrance, and when he couldn't find the car, he called home and said it had been stolen. He was really upset. Dad and I, we borrowed a neighbor's car and drove to the shopping center and picked Ben up. Then we drove him all around the parking lot until we found our car. We sure had a good laugh over that, but Benny didn't think it was funny."

I laughed too. But it sounded strange hearing him call my dad "Benny." "Tell me more stories about Dad when he was little," I said.

"When he was just a little kid, you mean, like you?" Now Uncle Charlie was grinning. We were stopped at a light, and he began to chuckle. "Well, once, I remember, he and Harold and Howard had a contest to see who could open his mouth the widest, and your dad won . . ."

I smiled.

". . . and ended up going to the hospital," Uncle Charlie finished.

"*What?*" I said.

"Seems he opened it so wide, the jawbone slipped out of place and he couldn't close his mouth. Mom had to take him to the emergency room. He was mad at me that day, though, because as they left the house, I hollered after him that he'd better put a screen over his door or else the flies would get in."

Now we both were laughing out loud.

"But most of the time," Uncle Charlie said, "your dad and I got along just fine."

"Did you still like each other when you both fell in love with Mom?" I asked.

"*What?*" cried Uncle Charlie, and he almost put on the brakes.

"I—I thought you loved my mom first and Dad stole her away from you," I said, trying to remember an old family story.

"Aha! That was another Charlie—a guy by the name of Charlie Snow. That's right, I'd almost forgotten. Your mom did have another boyfriend before she married Ben. You'll have to ask your dad about that sometime."

At the rental shop we picked up Uncle Charlie's tuxedo.

"One more stop," he said as he started the car up again. "I have to pick up the wedding rings."

"You don't even have the rings yet?" I asked.

"Oh, yes. But we couldn't decide what to have engraved inside them. We just made up our minds last week," he said.

I didn't think anyone could engrave words inside a tiny gold band. The rings were waiting, though, in their white velvet box, and the clerk shook Uncle Charlie's hand and said, "Congratulations." Then he looked at me and said, "You make sure your grandpa behaves himself, now."

When we got out to the car, I said, "Do I have to take care of Grandpa at the wedding?"

Uncle Charlie laughed. "Oh, no. He meant me."

"*You're* not my grandpa!" I said.

"No, but I'm old enough to be," he told me. "All the McKinley brothers married late, I guess. I'm just your extra-old uncle who's getting himself married at the grand age of fifty-seven." Then, before he started the car again, he said, "If you can keep a secret, Alice, you can read what's engraved inside the rings. Nobody knows but Marge and me."

I looked at him. "Sure!" I said.

"You won't tell a soul?"

I shook my head.

He opened the box, and I took out the largest ring—his—and turned it around and around until I could read the writing on the inside. It said, *Forever. Mousie.*

"Mousie?" I said.

"That's my pet name for Marge. She's saying she'll be mine forever."

I put it back and picked up the smaller ring for Aunt Marge. I had to squint to read the words because they were so tiny. *Forever. Chums.*

"And that's her sweet-talking word for me," Uncle

Charlie said, and smiled. "We're just two old fools having the best time of our lives and getting married."

"I think it's wonderful, Uncle Charlie," I said. "And I hope you're happy forever and ever."

And I wondered if someday I might be saying that to my dad.

I thought I had picked a nice dress for the wedding, but when I came downstairs on Saturday, everyone stopped talking and stared at me.

"*What?*" I said, stopping on the bottom step and looking myself over. I had on my velvet dress and my best tights without any holes in them and my patent leather shoes. I thought I looked great.

"You're wearing *black!*" said Dad. "You don't wear black to a wedding, sweetheart."

"Why?" I said. I was ready to burst into tears. It was the only dress I'd brought with me.

Aunt Vivian came over and put her arms around me. "Darlin', don't you mind them one bit. You look perfectly fine to me," she said. "We'll just add a pink sash to that dress and put on a white lace collar, and y'all be the prettiest one at the wedding, next to the bride."

By the time Aunt Vivian and Aunt Linda got through with me, I looked like a piece of licorice candy dipped in strawberries. There was a pink ribbon in my hair, a white lace collar around my neck, and a pink sash around my waist, with little bunches of fake roses tied to the straps of my Mary Janes.

All I'd done was reach into my closet for something Aunt Sally had sent me, clothes that Carol had outgrown, and grabbed something fancy. A mother would have told me I shouldn't wear black. I wanted to bawl.

By the time we got to the church, though, I'd lost the flowers off both straps of my shoes, and when the ceremony was over, I noticed that the bow had fallen out of my hair, and I felt better. At the reception I got rid of the pink sash, so all that was left was the white lace collar, and I decided I could live with that.

Uncle Charlie danced with Aunt Marge, and I danced with Dad; Dad danced with Aunt Vivian and Aunt Linda, and I danced with Lester. Uncle Harold and Uncle Howard both made toasts to their brother and said it was about time Charlie got married. Then Dad made a toast to Uncle Charlie and wished him and Marge health and happiness. And then we heard Grandpa McKinley say, "Where's the doggone wedding cake? That's what I came for," and everyone laughed.

Uncle Charlie and Aunt Marge changed clothes, and then we were all going to the airport to see them off on their honeymoon.

"Alice darlin'," said Uncle Harold, "do you think you

could entertain your grandfather while we pack up the wedding presents to take back to the house later? Your aunts are busy packing up the cake and punch."

"Sure," I said, not at all sure, but I walked over to where Grandpa McKinley sat scowling in his wheelchair and sat down next to him. He turned his head and gave me a ferocious stare.

"I *said* I wanted to go home," he told me. "I'm not gettin' on any cockeyed airplane."

"You're not going on an airplane, Grandpa. Uncle Charlie and Aunt Marge are getting on. We're just going along to tell them good-bye."

"So what's wrong with their car?" he asked.

I blinked. Sometimes it's hard to follow Grandpa. "Nothing. But I don't think you can drive a car to Bermuda," I said.

"Eh?" he said.

I put my mouth to his ear. "I don't think you can drive to Bermuda," I shouted.

"That's what's wrong with cars today, they don't hold up. Won't go anywhere," Grandpa shouted back at me.

I tried to think how to quiet him down. "What kind of a car did you used to have?" I asked. "What was your first car, Grandpa?"

That seemed to be the magic button. Grandpa McKinley settled back in his wheelchair and began to smile. "I had a 1927 Model T Roadster," he said. "A Ford Roadster." And he smiled some more.

"What did the car have?" I asked.

"Why, it had headlamps, a horn, a starter, a hand-operated windshield wiper, windshield wings. . . . It had bumpers, front and rear, and a rearview mirror, shock absorbers, and it came with five wire wheels. Yessir, that car had everything!"

By the time Uncle Howard came to get Grandpa, Grandpa McKinley was on his third car, a Model A Fordor sedan, and I heard afterward that he talked about cars all the way to the airport and all the way back.

On our drive back to Maryland, we all said we were glad we had come, even Lester. I was remembering how happy Chums and Mousie looked as they went down the ramp to the plane and how I was the only one who knew what was engraved on their wedding rings.

But something horrible happened. Two days later, when we were back in Takoma Park, we got word that Uncle Charlie had died of a heart attack on his honeymoon.

It was so awful—so sudden. My dad just put his forehead against the wall and cried, and that made me cry too. I pressed my face against Dad's hand and sobbed.

Lester went up to his room and closed his door.

We drove to Tennessee all over again the following weekend for the funeral. Lester and I didn't complain at all this time, and we didn't ask for any more bathroom stops than we had to. Once I looked over at Dad and saw tears in his eyes again. Then I choked up.

"I'm r-really sorry, Dad, about Uncle Charlie," I said softly.

"Yeah, me too," said Lester, and he wasn't even listening to his Walkman. "Life really stinks sometimes."

"Yes," said Dad. "Life can be *very* rough sometimes." He paused, then said, "You just have to keep going. To wade through it. You can't go around."

The funeral dinner was held in the very same room where we'd had the wedding reception the week before, and I was wearing the same black velvet dress. In fact, the lemon sponge cake looked a lot like the leftover wedding cake with a little lemon sauce poured over it, and instead of everyone giving their best wishes to Aunt Marge, they were all crying and hugging her, and she was crying too.

"Aunt Marge, I'm so sorry," I wept.

"So am I," she told me. "We had two wonderful days, Alice. Two wonderful days, but that was all."

"Where's Charlie?" Grandpa kept asking.

"He died, Dad," my father told him for about the fifteenth time.

"Died?" said Grandpa. Then he got very quiet. He still didn't understand, I guess. It was hard to explain things to Grandpa.

We stayed in Tennessee until Monday, and when we left to go home, Aunt Marge gave all of us big hugs, and Grandpa even let me kiss him on the cheek. I decided that hugs could go a long, long way toward making you feel better.

We were pretty quiet on the way home to Maryland, but there were tears in my eyes the whole way.

"Can honeymoons kill you?" I asked Dad.

"Usually they make you feel better, not worse," said Dad.

"Did you and Mom have a honeymoon?" I wanted to know.

"Yes. We went camping," said Dad.

"That's a *honeymoon?*" asked Lester.

"It was all we could afford at the time, Les, and it was enough. We had each other," Dad said.

"Poor Uncle Charlie," I said. "Poor Aunt Marge." For Chums and Mousie, "forever" turned out to be only two days.

10

The Sad Time

I told Rosalind about Uncle Charlie's funeral when I went back to school on Tuesday. We were sitting on the steps, waiting for the bell, and were trying to figure out why a man would die on his honeymoon.

"Maybe his wife was a bad cook," said Rosalind. "Maybe what she cooked was so awful, it killed him."

And when I didn't say anything, she added, "Or maybe he'd been a bachelor for so long that when his wife saw him in his underpants, he died of embarrassment." Finally she said, "I'm never going to get married."

"Maybe I won't either," I told her. "I don't think I could ever love a boy as much as I love my cat."

"Then marry a tomcat and have kittens," said Rosalind, and we laughed.

The Terrible Triplets were coming up the sidewalk.

"What's so funny?" said Megan.

"None of your beeswax," said Rosalind. And then she said, "Honeymoons."

"Honeymoons?" said Jody. "Is that where Alice was yesterday?"

And then it started all over again. "Hey, everybody, Alice and Donald went on a honeymoon!" Dawn yelled.

All the kids came running over to the steps and shouted that silly chant:

> "Alice and Don-ald,
> Sitting in a tree,
> K-I-S-S-I-N-G."

Everybody looked at me to see if I was getting mad. I couldn't stand it. I couldn't stand all that teasing and hollering and kissing business. I didn't want to have to tell them about the funeral, either, because I was afraid I might start to cry; but I had to stop them somehow, and suddenly I heard myself saying, "It wasn't me who went on a honeymoon, it was my uncle. And guess what? He was murdered."

Rosalind jerked around and stared at me.

"What?" said Megan. "Really?"

"I just got back from the funeral," I said, and all the kids stopped grinning.

"Who killed him?" asked Dawn.

"We don't know yet. The police are still investigating," I said. Inside, my stomach felt like a rock. How could I do this to Uncle Charlie?

"I'll bet his new wife poisoned him," said a skinny boy named Ollie Harris.

I swallowed. How could I do this to Aunt Marge?

"I'll bet she smothered him in his sleep," said somebody else.

"I'm never going to get married, ever!" said Donald Sheavers, which suited me fine, but I still felt sick to my stomach.

The bell rang, and kids were still talking about the murder when we went inside.

"He *wasn't*, was he? Murdered?" Rosalind whispered to me.

"Well, he didn't kill *himself*," I answered miserably.

It was about ten o'clock and we were having a spelling test when the principal's voice came over the loudspeaker. "Excuse the interruption, Mrs. Burstin, but could you send Alice McKinley to my office? Thank you."

I think my heart stopped beating for a moment. If you are called to the principal's office, it means one of two things: you are in deep, deep doo-doo, or something awful has happened at home.

Mrs. Burstin nodded to me, meaning I could get up

and leave, and I was so scared that I had to stop in the rest room before I went to the office.

"Go right in there, Alice," the school secretary said when I walked in the door.

There was Mr. Serio behind the desk.

"Hello, Alice," he said. "Sit down." He got up and closed the door behind me, but the secretary could still see us through the glass window. I swallowed.

"I understand that your family's been through quite an ordeal," he said quietly. He sat back in his chair and folded his fingers over his stomach. "First your uncle got married, then he died. I'm really very sorry."

"S-So am I," I said.

"When your father asked if you could miss a day of school to go back for the funeral, Alice, he told me that your uncle died of a heart attack," Mr. Serio went on. "So I was very surprised when reports reached me this morning that he was murdered. That is terrible news, isn't it?"

"I—I guess so," I said.

"Alice," said Mr. Serio, "what made you say that? Why did you tell the other kids that your uncle was murdered?"

How could I tell the principal that I made up the story to stop all that kissing stuff?

"Well . . . well . . . *something* killed him, didn't it? I didn't say a *person* killed him," I explained, stumbling over my words.

Mr. Serio just kept looking at me. He wasn't exactly smiling, but he wasn't frowning, either. "I think you know the difference, Alice. You're a smart girl. So tell me why you needed to say that."

I could already feel tears rolling out of the corners of my eyes. "B-Because the kids were t-teasing me about D-Donald and honeymoons, and the Terrible Triplets were making fun of—"

"The who?"

"The three witches," I said.

"Alice, are you having trouble making friends here?" asked Mr. Serio.

"No, I'm making lots of friends," I said suddenly, not wanting anybody to feel sorry for me. "Except for the Terrible Triplets, and *they're* having trouble making friends with *me!*"

"I see," said Mr. Serio. "Well, I think that somehow you have to let them know that your uncle died of a heart attack, that he wasn't murdered. But I'll leave it to you to figure out just *how* you're going to tell them."

"Okay," I said.

At recess everyone gathered around. They wanted to know why I was called into Mr. Serio's office.

"We found out what killed my uncle," I said.

"You mean he wasn't murdered?" everyone asked.

"Well, I can tell you this much: He died of a heart attack. And you know what can give you a heart attack? A terrible, terrible shock! If someone scares you bad enough, your heart will just stop beating."

"Who scared him enough to give him a heart attack?" asked Jody.

"We don't know. They're still investigating," I said, and hoped that would be the end of it.

For a while I was feeling sad about everything. Sad about Uncle Charlie and sad for my new Aunt Marge and sad for my dad because he'd lost his favorite brother. On top of everything else, the milkman knocked on our door and told us that his company was going to stop home deliveries at the end of the year. All the other companies had stopped delivering milk years ago, and from now on, we'd have to buy our milk at the store like everyone else. What's more, he was out of a job. After thirty-one years with the company, he said, he had nowhere to go in the mornings.

He looked so sad when he told us that I could hardly stand it. On the last day he came by to pick up the bottles, I wrote a poem and stuck it down inside one of the empties. Here's what I wrote:

> *There are lots of drops in the ocean,*
> *There are lots of stars in the blue,*
> *But in the whole state of Maryland,*
> *There's only one person like you.*
> Alice McKinley, age 8

I don't know if he ever read it. Maybe he just dumped all the empties into the big bottle-washing machine and the paper went down the drain. But who says he didn't put it in a scrapbook to treasure always?

Aunt Sally and Uncle Milt decided that we shouldn't be alone on our first Christmas away from relatives. So Aunt Sally called to say that they were coming to Maryland for Christmas, ready or not, and I guess that was just what we needed. Because Aunt Sally just takes over when she's in someone's house. Dad let her and Uncle Milt have his bed. He slept on an old army cot in the basement with Lester, and Carol slept in my bed. I slept on the floor in my sleeping bag.

Before we knew it, a tree went up in the living room, and Aunt Sally set to work in the kitchen making pies and rolls and apple dumplings. Presents were piled under the tree, a wreath appeared on the door, and Dad even sat down at the piano one evening and played Christmas carols while the rest of us sang. Well, everyone but me. Lester said he would give me a quarter *not* to sing, so I figured I might as well make some money off it.

"Okay, Alice, you're next," said Carol when she'd finished trimming the tree. "We have to decorate you for Christmas."

I giggled.

"First, your nails," she said. She painted every other nail green and the rest of them red. She braided a large red ribbon in my hair and put silver sparkles on my eyelids. We went downstairs to show Lester.

"Look how beautiful I am!" I crowed, leaning closer so he could see my face.

"Great! Go hang yourself on the tree," he said.

But it was fun having Carol around. We sat up late at night playing cards, and Dad took us all to the *Messiah* Sing-Along at a church on Cedar Lane. This time Lester said he would pay me a *dollar* not to sing and embarrass him, but I couldn't have anyway, because I can't read music. I just wanted to be in the same room with all the people singing, "Hallelujah! Hallelujah! Hal-leeeee-lu-jah!" And that's exactly what I did.

11

The World According
to Rosalind

Uncle Milt and Aunt Sally and Carol went home a few days after Christmas, but on New Year's Day, the Naked Nomads met in our basement again to practice. Rosalind came with her brother. She brought along a 500-piece jigsaw puzzle of a jungle, and we sat around our huge living-room coffee table putting the pieces together.

"I wish we never had to go back to school," said Rosalind. She was working on the zebra, while I was looking for the last two pieces of the giraffe.

"Oh, it's not that bad," I said. "Some parts of it are okay."

"Which parts?" asked Rosalind.

"Lunch and recess," I said, and we laughed.

"Not the Terrible Triplets," said Rosalind.

"No, not them," I told her.

"The next time they try to eat at our table, we should say, 'No triplets allowed,'" said Rosalind.

I put the hind legs on the giraffe.

"The next time they ask me if I live in the elephant house, I'll say, 'Yes, right next to you, the hippos,'" said Rosalind.

I found the tip of the giraffe's tail and started work on the panda bear.

"The next time one of them needs a partner for anything, we'll say, 'Sorry. Try the monkey house,'" said Rosalind. She hated the Terrible Triplets even more than I did, because of the way they called her an elephant.

"If I were queen of the world, you know what I'd do? Make everybody change places," Rosalind went on, picking up a puzzle piece with the face of a gorilla on it and slapping it down hard with the palm of her hand. "Everybody who's skinny would have to be fat, and everybody who's rich would have to be poor, and everyone would have to be kind to animals."

I thought about that. "If I were queen—no, if I were God—I wouldn't let anyone die until they were a hundred years old," I said. "I especially wouldn't let a man die on his honeymoon or a mother die before her children were all grown up."

That settled, we furiously attacked the puzzle, seeing who could find the next piece the fastest and slapping each one down hard with our hands.

• • •

Here's what I like:
    500-piece jigsaw puzzles
    Rosalind
    My cousin Carol
    Anything with chocolate
    Macaroni and cheese
    My cat

Here's what I hate:
    The Terrible Triplets
    People dying
    Maps of the United States
    War
    Gas-station rest rooms

Lester gave me a black-and-white notebook with lined paper in it that he'd never used, and I began keeping my lists in that. I wanted to see if, when I got to be twenty, I still loved and hated the same things I do now.

When I went back to school after New Year's, the Terrible Triplets were all wearing new sweaters that were exactly alike. They weren't even sisters, but they'd got their mothers to buy them red sweaters with little white reindeer on them. Whenever we changed classes—went to the gym or anything—they linked arms and walked down the hall in step.

At lunchtime, when they came to our table, Rosalind put her feet on the two chairs across from her and said that all the chairs were taken. When we paired up for relay races and Dawn and Megan chose each other, Jody looked around for a partner, and Rosalind told her to try the monkey house. When Megan asked if she could borrow my blue pen to draw in the Mississippi River on her map, Rosalind reached over and took my pen for herself.

"We don't loan things to triplets," she said.

I went on working, but across the aisle Megan was sitting so still that I stole a look at her. I thought she'd be glaring at Rosalind and me, but she was just staring down at her paper, and she looked *sad*. Really sad! I felt a hollow thunk in my chest, but when I looked over at her again, Megan had turned the other way. Now I had *two* things to feel bad about: what I'd said about Uncle Charlie and what we had done to Megan.

I wasn't so sure about Rosalind. It seemed to me she just liked to keep a war going.

At dinner that night, Dad and Lester were talking about the fighting in the Middle East and about how, when there's so much hate going around, the slightest thing can start a fight.

"Is that how wars begin?" I asked. "Somebody says something mean, and then *that* person says something back, and before you know it, they're fighting?"

"Sort of," said Lester.

"And it ends when they all make up?" I asked.

"Usually when one side runs out of bullets or soldiers and they just give up," Lester said.

That got me thinking about the Terrible Triplets. I imagined our quarrel ending only when all five of us—Dawn and Jody and Megan and Rosalind and I—were lying dead on the playground.

At school the next day, I was the last one to the table with my tray, and there was only one seat left. Both Dawn and Jody put their feet on it and said it was reserved for triplets only. I had to go to the boys' table and eat with Donald Sheavers.

At recess they got the jump rope first and wouldn't let me in. Rosalind either.

"See how they act?" said Rosalind. "They *want* us to hate them."

Maybe she was right; I didn't know.

At least I had Rosalind for a friend. The girl with the dirty hair didn't seem to have anybody. I thought about telling her to wash her hair and chew with her mouth closed and then I'd be her friend, but that didn't sound quite right. She was smart, though. Her name was Sara, and she said funny things sometimes that made people laugh.

We were learning to write letters and signing them *Yours truly,* and then we had to read them to the class. Sara wrote a letter to her grandmother. She had the right margins and she had put the date in the right place, but instead of *Yours truly,* she wrote, *Yours till the Mississippi wears rubber pants to keep its bottom dry.*

Everybody laughed. Mrs. Burstin laughed too. She said that sometimes people who like each other a lot sign their letters *Yours forever.* And Sara was saying *Yours forever* in another way, because the Mississippi River would never wear rubber pants. I decided right then I liked Sara, even though I didn't like her hair.

But when I told Rosalind I thought Sara was funny, she said, "I'm still your best friend, aren't I?"

Donald Sheavers was my friend too, though. He said my cat was lonely. He said she liked being with Killer while we were in Tennessee, so I told him I would bring her over if we could call Killer "Muffin" while I was there.

I don't know if Muffin could even see Oatmeal or not, but he could smell her. She would pounce on his paws and swat at his tail, and Killer—I mean, Muffin—would go rooting around the rug, trying to sniff out Oatmeal with his nose. Even if he was deaf, I'll bet he could have heard her purr, because Oatmeal purrs so loud.

I didn't like to think of my kitten as lonely. But I especially didn't like the thought that Donald had been right, that the dog and cat went together as well as muffins and oatmeal. But this was a war I could stop before it even began.

"Okay, you were right," I said. "Muffin and Oatmeal get along fine. I'd just feel better if we called your dog 'Muffin' from now on."

"You can call him anything you want," said Donald. "He can't hear you anyway."

I told Rosalind about Oatmeal and Muffin. We were sitting on the swings on the playground. It had snowed the night before, and we let our boots drag in it as we twisted the swings around and around, making circles on the ground when the swings began to unwind.

"Maybe they'll have babies," she said.

I stared at Rosalind. "They *can't* have babies!" I told her. "One is a dog and one's a cat!"

"Well, what's a mule, then?" she asked.

"What's that got to do with anything?" I wanted to know.

"Is a mule a horse or a donkey?"

"I don't know. Part horse, part donkey, I guess," I said.

"See?" said Rosalind. "If horses and donkeys can

make mules, then why can't dogs and cats make . . . um . . . I don't know . . . dats or cogs or something."

"Rosalind, you are weird sometimes," I told her.

"I know," said Rosalind, grinning at me over the snow. "That's why we're best buddies. Right?"

12

Starting with Me

It was around the first of February that I got sick. When Dad woke me to go to school, I walked down the hall to breakfast, got as far as the kitchen doorway, and threw up on my bare feet. And in case anybody wants to know, it was warm and looked like vegetable soup.

"Al!" yelled Lester, scooting his chair away from the table, as though my vomit had splashed his pants or something.

"I'm sorry," I said, and barfed again.

"Honey!" Dad exclaimed, clanking the pan of oatmeal back on the stove and hurrying over. He grabbed a paper towel and held it under my chin. That almost made me upchuck again, but I guess there wasn't anything left in my stomach. With his other hand, he felt my forehead.

"You're burning up," he said. "Let's get you right back to bed." He guided me down the hall and, over his shoulder, called, "Lester, get the mop, would you?"

"Dad!" Lester yelled in horror. "I'm still eating breakfast!"

"Not anymore, you're not," Dad said. "I need some help here. Now please get the mop." Lester gave a howl of pain.

Dad says Lester has a queasy stomach. Les can imagine himself having almost any kind of disease there is. Dad says if Lester ever went to work in a hospital, he'd be the first patient in the emergency room.

But right then I wasn't concerned about Lester. I was just trying to make it back to bed with legs as limp as cooked macaroni.

Dad gets very quiet and worried-looking when one of us gets sick. After I lay down again, propped up against my pillow, Dad brought in the thermometer and put it under my tongue; then he sat down on the edge of my bed and studied my face. You know what's weird? When somebody's taking your temperature and he just sits and looks at you. Like I'm supposed to *do* something. Make the thermometer hurry, maybe.

I wiggled my toes under the bedclothes and watched the ripples they made in the blanket. Then I spread my hands out on both knees to see if the fingernails on my right hand were as dirty as the nails on the left. I tried to imagine what would happen if I bit down on the thermometer and broke the glass and all the mercury came out in my mouth and I swallowed it and got mercury poisoning and died, and I knew that Aunt Sally would say we never should have left Chicago.

Finally, when it seemed ten minutes had gone by and Dad was looking past me out the window, I began to clear my throat.

"Oh! Right!" Dad said. He leaned over and took out the thermometer, then laid it on the back of his hand and slowly turned it around. "Oh," he said again softly.

"What is it, Dad?" I asked. Even my voice sounded weak and feeble.

"About a hundred and two," he said. "First I'm going to call the doctor. Then I'll call the store and tell them I won't be in today."

He went down the hall to the bathroom, came back with a wet washcloth, and put it on my forehead. Then he asked if I wanted orange juice or something. When he saw me clamp my lips together, as though I might throw up again, he said, "No, better not."

Something was different this time about my being sick, but I couldn't figure out what. Then I knew: It wasn't just the first time I'd been sick here in Takoma Park; it was the first time there was no one else around to take care of me except Dad. Even after Mom died, there was Aunt Sally, and whenever I had a cold or a fever, she'd come over and stay with me till Dad got home from work. Now it was just Dad and Lester and me, and we had to look out for each other.

My father kept going to the window and back again, waiting for the doctor to call, as though any minute he might drive right up to our house.

"Tell me everything that hurts, Alice," he said finally. "The doctor will want to know."

"My head hurts," I said. "And I ache all over."

"Is your throat sore? Do your ears hurt?"

I shook my head.

"Tummy ache?"

"A little."

The phone rang and Dad went into the living room to answer. When he came back, he said, "The doctor says he's quite sure you have what's going around, an intestinal flu—headache, vomiting, and fever. He had seven calls about it yesterday. He says there really isn't anything to do but take Tylenol and drink plenty of water. But you can't go back to school until your temperature's normal."

Dad sat by my bed and read the newspaper while I tried to sleep some more, but I couldn't. I lay still for a long time with my eyes closed, hating the feeling of wanting to vomit and not being able to. I guess I did sleep a little, though, because when I opened my eyes again, Dad had taken off his shoes and was leaning against the wall, with sofa pillows behind his back. He gently stroked my forehead.

"I remember," he said, "the day you were born." He looked down at me and smiled. "You hardly had any hair at all. Just peach fuzz, we called it. I told Marie that's what we ought to call you, Peach Fuzz, but she had a name all picked out—Alice. Like Alice in Wonderland, because you were such a wonder. After Lester was born, see, we'd wanted more children, but we just didn't have much luck. And then—when we'd almost given up hope of having another child—Marie was pregnant again with you."

Dad tipped his head back and went on stroking the side of my face. "We'd been close before, of course— Marie and Lester and I. But it wasn't till you came along—starting with Alice, I guess—that we began to feel that our family was complete."

I grinned. "Starting with me," I said.

"That's right. What we needed was a little girl, and we got the best little girl in the world."

"Yeah, but I can't sing," I said.

"Who cares?" said Dad.

"I've got freckles," I told him.

"All the better," he said.

"And I'm . . . I'm not always nice to Lester," I confessed.

"No, I suppose not. But if you were perfect, you

wouldn't be Alice, now, would you?" He adjusted the pillows behind his back, and then I saw that he'd brought some books along with him and they were strewn about the bedcovers. "How about if I read to you?" he said. "Your choice: *The Prince and the Pauper, Charlotte's Web,* or *Pinch*?"

"*The Prince and the Pauper,*" I said. "I've read the others."

"Ah! Mark Twain! My favorite!" said Dad, and began to read: "'In the ancient city of London, on a certain autumn day in the second quarter of the sixteenth century, a boy was born to a poor family of the name of Canty, who did not want him. On the same day another English child was born to a rich family of the name of Tudor, who did want him. All of England wanted him too. . . .'"

Every so often, my dad read aloud to us like this, and it was so wonderful, lying in bed, cozy and warm, listening to his voice, that I almost forgot I felt like throwing up.

I think I must have dozed off after the first chapter, though, because when I opened my eyes again, the room was dark. Dad had pulled the blinds down and gone back out to the living room. I didn't feel quite as bad as I had before, but I could tell I still had a fever.

I wondered what I was missing at school and how much work I'd have to make up when I got back.

Maybe Rosalind was sick too, and her brother had to mop up after her. Maybe the Triplets were all home too, throwing up on their matching red sweaters.

Then I got to thinking about the girl with the dirty hair and how I shouldn't think of her like that. She had a name: Sara. I wouldn't want to be remembered as the girl who couldn't sing. I'd just want to be known as Alice. The next time I saw her, I'd say, "Hi, Sara."

Then I got this terrific idea. If Rosalind and Sara and I became friends, we could be triplets too. We could be the *Terrific* Triplets. *We* could go around the playground with our arms around each other. We could all sit together at a table at lunch.

I decided that when I got better, I was going to have a sleep-over and invite Rosalind and Sara, and we would have a shampoo party and get in the bathtub, and then Rosalind and I could help Sara wash her hair and make her look better.

I heard the front door open and Lester coming down the hall. He poked his head in my bedroom. "How you feeling? Are you through barfing yet?" he asked.

"I don't know. Come a little closer and I'll see," I said.

"Not on your life," he told me. "Just let me know if you want a Coke or something, and I'll roll a can across the floor to you. Okay?"

I think Dad was right. Our family wasn't complete until I came along. Mom and Dad must have looked at Lester and decided, *No, we need a little bit more.*

And that little bit more was me.

13

The Shampoo Party

Lester got sick after I did. He said it was my germs that did it, but he was eating nachos again in two days, so he couldn't have been as sick as I was.

Four kids in my class had the flu—Donald Sheavers and Megan and two boys I hardly knew, so I don't think they got it from me. The main thing I missed was writing a report on an insect and reading it to the class. The day I came back to school, Sara read her report on the praying mantis.

Sara reads with a lot of expression, and what she told us . . . it was awful! About how the female eats the male after they mate. Just gobbles him right up. And then she rubbed her stomach and said, "Yum-yum!"

That made us laugh, but it was awful at the same time, and we looked at Mrs. Burstin.

"It's true, class," the teacher said. "Sara is exactly right. Very good research, Sara!"

"Man, I'm never getting married!" said Ollie Harris, and everybody laughed. That made four people in third grade who were never getting married!

"Don't worry, Ollie. You're not a bug," said Rosalind, and we laughed some more.

Sara laughed too.

I told Rosalind about my plan for the sleep-over, but she wasn't too crazy about the idea.

"Why do you want another best friend?" she asked. "I thought I was your best friend."

I had to think fast. "Because I thought the three of us could be triplets too. Megan and Dawn and Jody aren't the only ones who can be triplets."

"Sara's hair stinks," said Rosalind.

"That's why we'll make it a shampoo party, but we won't tell her why we're doing it. We don't want to embarrass her," I said.

"But we'll still be best friends, you and me?" asked Rosalind.

"Sure," I told her.

The good thing about being "best friends" is that you're supposed to tell each other all your secrets and help each other out of trouble. The bad thing about being best friends is you aren't supposed to like anyone else as much as you like each other. And if you talk to somebody else too much, your best friend gets jealous. But I decided that, for now, anyway, Rosalind could be my best friend.

We sat down across from Sara at lunch and talked some more about praying mantises. She said that her uncle was an entomologist—a person who studies bugs—and that's how she knew what the female praying mantis does.

"I'm going to have a sleep-over on Friday," I said. "Do you want to come? Rosalind will be there too."

"Okay," said Sara. She was eating a ham sandwich and chewing with her mouth open again. You could see the yellow mustard and the white bread and the green lettuce all mixed up together just inside her mouth. I looked at her eyes instead, which were deep blue.

"Don't you have to ask your mom first?" I said.

"She'll say yes," said Sara.

I found out where she lived and said we'd pick her up.

"Okay," said Sara.

Her face is as thin as Rosalind's is wide. She has thin lips and a pinched-in nose, and her long stringy hair makes her face look even thinner.

Megan and Dawn and Jody must have heard me talking about a sleep-over, because Dawn started talking a little too loud about a sleep-over *she* was going to have that weekend and how they were going to make taffy and teach each other to dance. I knew they were trying to make it sound like they were going to have a better sleep-over than we were just because I didn't invite them.

When Friday came, I got in the car with Dad, and we drove to the address Sara had given. It was a tiny house with a chain-link fence around it and toys in the yard. Dad went to the door with me and knocked.

Sara answered with three of her brothers, all crowding around staring at us. There were more kids on the couch watching TV. Sara's mother came out of the kitchen. She was wearing jeans and a sweatshirt with REDSKINS on it. She had the same thin face as Sara.

"Hello," said Dad. "I'm Ben McKinley, and I understand your daughter is coming to a sleep-over at our house. I thought I ought to give you our address and phone number."

"Yes, that's a good idea. I'm Bev Evans," said Sara's mother. She got a pencil and wrote down our address and phone number. "Do you have everything you need, Sara?" she asked.

Sara held up her canvas bag. "I think so."

"Have a good time," said her mother. "Behave yourself."

"I'm sure she will," said Dad.

All Sara's brothers and sisters crowded around the door and watched her leave. As we walked back out to the car, Sara said, "They're excited because they get to sleep in my bed tonight with Melody."

Dad laughed. "How many brothers and sisters do you have?"

"Six. I'm the third oldest, and I make seven. I sleep with Melody, but tonight Stephanie and Gayle get to take my place."

"Where do they sleep when you're home?" I asked.

"On the couch," she said simply, as though every family put some of their kids to bed on the couch.

I thought about Sara as we drove home. Maybe if there are seven children and their parents all living together in a tiny house, there's too much to do and too little room to keep everything as clean as you'd like. Or maybe washing your hair just isn't as important as other things you have to do.

By the time we got to our place, Rosalind's mother was just driving up, and Dad talked with her a few minutes while Rosalind and Sara and I ran into the house and down the hall to my bedroom. Sara and Rosalind started taking things out of their bags—pajamas and toothbrushes and books and stuff. Rosalind took out a huge jar of purple bubble bath.

"Let's use it all!" she said mischievously.

"All of it?" I said, and Sara started to grin.

"The whole thing! Just to see what happens!" said Rosalind, and we started to giggle.

But first we had a tea party on the coffee table in the

living room. Rosalind and I had it all planned. I had made little cracker-and-cream-cheese sandwiches with olives on top and chocolate marshmallow cookies and hot cocoa.

We used cups and saucers and even napkins, and pretended that we were having tea at the Plaza Hotel in New York City. I've never been to the Plaza. I've never even been to New York, but Rosalind says that's where you go to have a really fancy party, so we pretended we were ladies in evening gowns, and we held the handles of our cups with our pinkies sticking up in the air.

"Now, remember," Rosalind said to me as though she were my mother, "you have to chew with your mouth closed."

"Yes, Mother!" I said, and Sara laughed.

Rosalind daintily tasted her cocoa and put the cup back down, then gently bit into a cracker sandwich.

"Wipe your mouth, Alice," said Rosalind, "and try not to let crumbs fall in your lap."

"Yes, Mother," I said.

"Sara, keep your lips together. I don't want to see you digesting your food," Rosalind scolded.

"Yes, Mother," said Sara, and giggled some more.

One thing they *don't* allow at the Plaza, I'll bet, are little kittens jumping up on your lap and on the tea table. Oatmeal had to join the party, of course, and

Sara and Rosalind took turns holding her, pretending she was their baby. There was a string hanging out of Sara's sleeve, and every time she moved her hand on the table, Oatmeal jumped at the string.

After we'd finished our cracker sandwiches, Dad said we could make brownies, except that he would put them in the oven for us and take them out again.

"Let's put all kinds of stuff in them," said Rosalind.

"Like what?" I said.

"Peanut butter," said Rosalind.

"Raisins," said Sara. "And M&M's, if you have any."

I had a package left from Halloween, so we put raisins and M&M's in the batter, some butterscotch chips, a little coconut, and a big glob of peanut butter. Rosalind swirled it around.

"Ready!" I called, and Dad put the pan in the oven.

The house soon filled with a wonderful chocolately smell. Even Lester poked his head into the kitchen. "Hey! What smells?" he said.

"You!" I told him, and we laughed.

"What's cooking?" he wanted to know.

"Chocolate-butterscotch-raisin-peanut-butter-M&M's brownies," said Rosalind.

"With sardines," said Sara, and we laughed some more.

"I guess I'm not hungry after all," said Lester, and went down in the basement to practice his guitar.

While the brownies were baking, I got out my black-and-white notebook and showed Sara and Rosalind the lists of things I liked and hated.

Rosalind asked if she could write her own list in my notebook, and I gave her my green pen:

Things I like, by Rosalind Rodriquez
> *Animals*
> *Marshmallows*
> *My grandmother*
> *Jesus*
> *Cookie dough*

Things I hate, by Rosalind Rodriquez
> *People who don't like animals*
> *Megan, Dawn, and Jody*
> *Shrimp*
> *Having my picture taken*

When she was done, she handed the notebook and pen to Sara:

Things I like, by Sara Evans
> *Friends*
> *Rocky Road ice cream*
> *My sisters and brothers*

Bubble gum
Books about science

Things I hate, by Sara Evans

For a long time Sara couldn't seem to think of anything to write down. Finally she wrote just one word: *Teasing.*

I noticed that Sara didn't put any people in her hate column, and yet she didn't seem to have many friends at school. Until now, anyway.

The timer on the oven dinged, and Dad came into the kitchen to take the brownies out of the oven. They looked really weird. There were holes where the M&M's had sunk in, I guess, and the coconut stuck through on top like someone needing a haircut.

"Hmm," said Dad, looking them over. "Tell you what. Let them cool for a while, and then you girls have a taste. If you're still alive after ten minutes, I'll try one."

They weren't bad, actually. Too sweet, but the raisins gave them a good flavor. Sara thought we ought to write down the recipe and send it to a baking contest.

Lester ordered pizza for dinner, and Dad made a salad. We sat down at the table, and I saw Lester's eyes go from me to Sara to Rosalind and back to me again.

"So what have we here?" he said. "The Three Musketeers?"

"We're triplets," said Rosalind. Sara giggled.

"The *Terrific* Triplets," I told him.

"Oh no!" said Lester. "You mean I have to have three sisters instead of one? Three sisters like *Alice?*"

"It could be worse," I said. "You could have three sisters like Megan and Dawn and Jody."

"Or you could have a praying mantis for a sister," said Sara. Now even Dad was staring.

"You know what they *do*, don't you?" I said.

"Yes," said Dad. "They're not very nice to their husbands."

"We had to write reports on insects for school," I explained. "Sara wrote hers on the praying mantis, and Rosalind chose the black widow spider."

"And what are *you* going to write about?" Lester asked me. "Roaches? Ticks?"

I leaned across the table, right up to his face. "How about *fleas*, Lester?" I said, and everybody laughed.

Rosalind and I couldn't wait for the bubble bath, so we decided to take it early and then play cards in my room. The three of us crowded into the bathroom, took off our clothes, giggling, and wrapped ourselves in towels while the bathtub filled. Rosalind took the lid off the purple bubble bath and dumped the whole thing under the running water.

It was like a volcano. Suds piled up higher and higher, till they were crawling along the wall toward the ceiling and oozing out over the edge of the tub. We dropped our towels and climbed in, laughing and squealing, and we couldn't even see each other, only our faces peeking out from the suds. When we saw the bubbles creeping across the bathroom floor toward the toilet, we screamed and hooted some more.

Dad tapped on the door and we screamed again. He opened the door a crack, but he didn't come in.

"Alice?" he called. "Is everything okay in there?"

I was laughing too hard to answer.

Dad poked his head in. All he saw were three faces among the bubbles. "Good grief," he said. "Well, if anybody gets lost in there, let me know." And he went back out into the living room.

We had a great time. We slipped and slid around the bottom of the tub and bumped into each other, sort of swimming through the bubbles.

Then I got out my shampoo and we all lathered up. We turned our hair into spikes and then horns and then cones, and finally, when we were through with all the bubbles, I turned on the shower. We rinsed our hair and washed all the bubbles down the drain.

After we'd dried off and mopped up the floor, we put on our pajamas and, with towels around our heads, went back to my room and brushed our hair. Rosalind said she washes her hair every night. I didn't think that was true, but I said I washed mine two times a week. Sara didn't say anything. But Rosalind and I told her she had beautiful hair, especially when it was shiny like it was now—sort of chestnut colored with red in it. Sara just grinned and grinned when she saw herself in the mirror.

Dad brought in some popcorn and Sara taught us a card game, Speed. We played it on my bed.

Then we unrolled the two sleeping bags Dad had brought up from the basement and turned out all the lights except for a tiny night-light in one corner. Sara said she'd tell us a ghost story. I thought it was going to be "The Golden Arm" or something like that, but it wasn't. It was awful!

Sara made it up, I could tell, because it was about a girl's mother who turns into a praying mantis. First her arms dropped off and bony sticks appeared in their place. Then her legs dropped off and sticklike legs unfolded beneath her. One day when the girl came home from school, there were two humps on her mother's back that became wings, and the *next* time the girl came home, her mother's head had changed into a long bony face with huge eyes and giant teeth and . . .

Before Sara had even finished the story, Rosalind had crawled into my bed with me and then Sara crawled in too, and when morning came, we found we had slept all night all scrunched up together. It's a wonder no one fell out of bed.

Dad made waffles for us, and after my friends went home, I thought about Sara. Maybe if kids tease you, you just sort of get used to hanging out by yourself, and her imagination helped keep her company. Whatever, I liked having Sara for a friend, and I think Rosalind did too.

"How was the sleep-over?" Lester asked me later after Dad had driven the girls home. He was lying on the living-room rug with a pillow under his head, reading the comics. "What was all the screaming about last night? Did you poison the brownies?"

"We were swimming in bubbles," I said. And then, "Sara made up a story about this girl whose mother turns into a praying mantis. First her arms drop off and then her legs, and then she grows wings and these big teeth and . . ."

While I was talking, I saw Oatmeal come into the room, stepping daintily, one paw in front of the other. I saw her stop to rub up against a leg of the coffee table. Then she gently stepped up on Lester's stomach and began turning around and around, the way she does when she wants to settle down and nap.

I finished the story, but I didn't say anything about Oatmeal. Before, Lester would have pushed her off without even looking at her. He didn't push her off this time as she nestled down, but he didn't look at her, either. He didn't even pet her.

Oatmeal stayed anyway. Maybe she knew that although he couldn't love her yet, she was safe with him. Her eyes began to close and she started to purr.

14

K-I-S-S-I-N-G

At school I began to notice that Sara washed her hair more often. She smiled more, too. That made her look a lot better.

When we ate together in the lunchroom and Rosalind caught either of us chewing with our mouth open, she'd say, "Keep your lips together, Sara," or, "I don't want to see you digesting your food, Alice," and we'd giggle and say, "Yes, Mother."

Of course, the next thing coming up at school was the Valentine's Day party. Megan and Dawn and Jody gave each other miniature boxes of Russell Stover chocolates and pretended they didn't know who they were from.

We all got valentines from Mrs. Burstin, and we had pink punch to drink and little paper cups filled with candies with words on them: HOT LIPS or I DIG YOU or OH, BABY!

When Mrs. Burstin wasn't looking, the boys tossed their candies at the girls they liked and some of the girls tossed them back. A couple of candies hit me on the side of my head, but I couldn't tell who had thrown them. They were probably meant for someone else.

Mrs. Burstin was glad to get rid of us at recess, I'll bet, and sent us outside even though it was cold. We put on our jackets and caps and stood shivering on the steps.

The kids who hadn't thrown their valentine candies around inside the classroom were whacking each other with them now, and every time a candy landed on the sidewalk, one of the boys would stamp on it as hard as he could and smush it into the cement.

There was a lot of giggling and whispering and punching going on among the boys, I noticed, and they kept trying to push each other toward the steps where some of us girls were trying to keep warm.

All at once a blond boy named Cory Schwartz was pushed right over at me until he practically fell in my lap. His lips sort of puckered up, and in a split second I rolled away from him down the steps, scrambled to my feet, and started to run.

Everyone was shouting and laughing. They sounded

like a cage of screaming monkeys at the zoo.

"Kiss her, Cory! Kiss her!" the boys bellowed.

I didn't know where to go. I ran as fast as I could, around the building, all the boys running after me, Cory in the lead, and everyone bellowing, "Kiss her, Cory! Kiss her!"

Not again! This couldn't be happening! Was this what third grade was all about? All this stupid kissing? I hardly even knew Cory Schwartz! I didn't even know he liked me. He probably didn't! Maybe he was doing it on a dare, and if he caught me and kissed me, I'll bet he'd tell everyone my breath smelled like rotten eggs.

The boys were getting closer and closer, and I didn't know where to go. I remembered a side door near the parking lot and wondered if I could get in the school there, so I turned the corner, and . . . POW!

I collided with something a lot bigger than me, and the next thing I knew, we both went sprawling. It was the huge patrol girl, who already hated my guts.

"You stupid jerk!" she yelled. "What do you think you're doing?" She winced and grabbed the palm of her left hand, which had been scraped on the gravel.

Here came the boys, but here came a teacher, too, who had seen the collision, and suddenly all the boys skidded to a stop.

"What happened?" asked the fifth-grade teacher, coming over.

"She just plowed right into me. Didn't even look where she was going," the patrol girl said, glaring at me as she got to her feet. Her shoulders were so broad, I'll bet she could have been a football player if she'd wanted.

"I think I'm going to be sick," I told the teacher.

She pointed to the side door. "Why don't you go in there and check in at the office. Let the school secretary look you over," she said.

I didn't go to the office because I was afraid the patrol girl would come in next to have her hand bandaged, so I hid in the girls' rest room till the bell, and then I was the first one in our classroom before the other kids came in. The boys were still laughing and giggling, and Cory was looking at me and grinning. Even Donald Sheavers was smiling. I tried to stare straight ahead.

"What are you going to *do,* Alice?" Rosalind whispered as she passed me.

"Move to Alaska," I told her.

It was like all the joy had gone out of my life. I would never be able to come to school early because Cory would be waiting for me there on the playground. I would have to sit as far away from him in the lunchroom as I could so that I'd be able to see him coming if he tried to kiss me. At recess I'd have to stay near the teacher all the time.

"You could always just bop him on the nose," Sara suggested.

"We'll be your bodyguards, Alice," said Rosalind.

That made me feel a little better, but they couldn't be bodyguards forever. If Cory had been dared to kiss me, he wouldn't stop trying. And sometime, when I didn't expect it, it would happen. Just the thought was so embarrassing I had to close my eyes to get rid of it.

At least he went one direction when school was out and I went another. That helped a little. But then I remembered the patrol girl at the entrance to the school driveway.

"Hey, you!" she yelled when she saw me, and I noticed she had a large Band-Aid on the palm of her hand. "Do you know you made me tear a hole in my jacket?"

I didn't know what to say, so I didn't say anything.

"I've got my eye on you!" she told me.

I hardly ate any dinner that evening.

"You're not sick again, are you?" asked Dad.

"If you're going to barf, baby, don't do it on the table," said Lester.

I stuck my fork in the top of my mashed potatoes and left it there. "I'm sick of life," I said.

"Really?" said Dad. "You've only been on this planet for eight years, and you're sick of it already?"

"I'm sick of third grade and I'm sick of Valentine's parties and I'm sick of boys and I'm especially sick of kissing," I said.

"Aha!" said Lester. "Why do I get the feeling that this must have been *some* Valentine's Day at school!"

"It was awful!" I said, my eyes beginning to fill with tears. "Cory Schwartz tried to kiss me because the other boys dared him to, and I was trying to get away, and I knocked over the biggest, meanest patrol girl in the whole school. Now *she's* got her eye on me, and *Cory's* waiting to kiss me, and the Terrible Triplets gave Russell Stover chocolates to each other and nobody gave chocolates to me!" I threw back my head and bellowed at the ceiling: "I hate third grade!"

"This, too, shall pass," said Dad.

"And I'm sick of hearing you say that!" I yelled. It seems that whenever Lester and I complain about something, Dad says, "This, too, shall pass." Sure, when I'm ninety years old or something.

"Alice, you're just an eight-year-old girl! You've got a lot of living yet to do," said Dad.

"I'm not just an eight-year-old girl, Daddy! Cory's out to get me! The patrol girl's out to get me! I'm like a . . . a hunted rabbit! A sitting duck! A cornered mouse!" I bleated.

"You sound more like a sheep to me," said Lester.

I went to my room after dinner and lay on my bed, holding a pillow to my tummy.

When Lester came out of the bathroom later, he looked in on me and said, "Are you really worried about this, Al?"

"Yes! I am really, really worried!" I said. "I can't stand thinking that Cory's going to jump out at me sometime and kiss me in front of everybody."

Lester came in and sat down on the edge of my bed. "Okay, I'll tell you what to do," he said. "There's only one thing *to* do, really. To Cory, anyway."

"Sock him?" I said.

"Nope. Kiss him first."

"What?" I sat up so fast, I knocked the pillow to the floor.

"Yep. Only way to stop it. Make *Cory* afraid of *you*. Hide behind the coats in the hallway or something, and when he comes by, just grab him and say, 'You want it? You got it.' Then kiss him."

"I can't!" I said. "I don't even like him. I don't even *know* him!"

"Well, you can't not like him if you don't even know him," said Lester. "You either kiss him first, or you go the rest of third grade looking over your shoulder and feeling like a hunted rabbit, a sitting duck, a . . . what was the other thing?"

"A cornered mouse," I said. I reached for the pillow and held it against my stomach again as Lester went down to the basement to do his homework.

I woke up early the next morning thinking about it. I gulped down a handful of dry Cheerios and a piece of banana. Then I brushed my teeth twice, gargled with Scope, and set off for school.

All the kids were gathered over by the school steps, waiting for the bell. When Donald Sheavers saw me coming, he nudged Cory Schwartz, and all the boys turned to look at me.

I didn't stop. I forced my feet to keep going—left, right, left, right—my heart keeping time with my feet. Everyone turned and stared. I didn't take my eyes off Cory Schwartz, and I don't know if I imagined it or not, but I think he took a step backward.

But when I was about two feet in front of him, I stopped, put my hands on my hips, and said, "Okay, Cory Schwartz, you wanted to kiss me. Go ahead and get it over with."

The boys whooped and hollered. The girls just stared. Cory Schwartz grew as red in the face as the punch at our Valentine's Day party. Somebody pushed him forward, and his mouth slid past my cheek and missed my ear. Then it was Cory Schwartz who was running away, around the building, with all the kids after him, shrieking and laughing. It would be Cory Schwartz hiding out in the boys' rest room from *me*, Cory Schwartz avoiding *me* on the playground, sitting as far away from me in the school lunchroom as he could possibly get.

I felt as though I were ten feet tall.

"Good for you, Alice!" said Sara.

"You did it!" said Rosalind.

"I *did*, didn't I?" I said.

✿ ✿ 15 ✿ ✿

Little Girl Lost

At school Jody, Dawn, and Megan were still snubbing us and we were snubbing them. It was getting a little boring, to tell the truth. The weird part was, I couldn't remember exactly how it had all begun. Had they started it or had we?

"You know what?" I said to Rosalind one day at lunch. "If we have to go the rest of the year like this, it's almost as bad as trying to hide from Cory Schwartz. If we go on being rude to them, they'll always want to get even."

"They'll never get even with us, because however rude they are to us, we'll think of something worse," said Rosalind.

"That's what I mean," I said.

• • •

When spring vacation came, Lester complained because Dad said he had to either stay home with me or take me with him wherever he went.

"Dad, this isn't fair!" Lester bellowed. "She's not my right leg or anything! No one else has to drag a sister around with him!"

"I know it's not fair, Lester, but until I can figure out how to work things here, that's the way it has to be. I don't want Alice home alone, and I won't ask Mrs. Sheavers to let her stay over there all the time. Things are a little rough right now, but we're doing the best we can."

"Well, I don't think we are," said Lester. "I've got a life to live, too, you know."

He finally decided that the only place he'd be willing to take me with him was the National Air and Space Museum at the Smithsonian. But since I wanted to see mummies and things, he said we could spend the morning at the National Museum of Natural History and the afternoon at Air and Space. Dad dropped us off at the metro that morning, and Lester bought fare cards for both of us.

As we left Silver Spring and sped along underground, Lester said, "When we get to Metro Center, we have to change to another line, and I want you to stick close to me."

"Why?" I asked.

"Because we could get separated in the crowd. I might get off and you'd stay on," he said.

I tried to imagine me with my nose pressed up against the window glass, watching my brother race along the platform, calling my name. I'd probably get off at the next stop, thinking Lester would come after me, but what if he didn't? What if I was the only one who got off and this evil-looking woman kidnapped me and locked me in her house and made me do all her work and only gave me bread and bones to eat? What if she chained me up at night and there wasn't any telephone and I couldn't see out because all the windows were painted black and . . .

"Lester," I said, "if I was ever missing, would you put my face on a milk carton?"

Lester looked over at me. "What?"

"You know . . . if I was a missing child or something."

"Well, let me think," said Lester. "A milk carton, huh? Quart size or half gallon?"

"Lester."

"Chocolate or two percent?"

"Lester!"

"Frontal view or side view?" asked Lester.

I just folded my arms over my chest and scowled.

Lester smiled and gave me a nudge. "Sure," he said.

I hung on to his jacket when we changed trains, and then we rode to the Smithsonian stop. You come right out on what's known as the Mall when you go up the escalator. Not a shopping mall, but the long grassy park that stretches between the Capitol and the Lincoln Memorial. The Smithsonian museums are along both sides.

Lester was very patient with me as I looked at the blue whale and the mummies and stuff. We saw the caveman exhibits and the hunters and gatherers and early man, and we were halfway through the next exhibit when I had to go to the bathroom.

"Lester, I need the rest room," I said. "I know where it is."

"You sure?"

I nodded.

"Okay, I'll meet you right here," he said.

I walked back through the exhibits to the hallway and turned left. I thought I'd seen the women's room right out there, but it wasn't. It was as though someone had moved it! I went on down the corridor till I came to the exhibit on Pacific cultures, and then I realized that we had come down the escalator and that the rest room was on the floor above us. I took the escalator up and turned left, but it still wasn't there, so I turned left again, and then I saw it. I went in there, but when I came out and tried to find Lester again, I was so mixed up, I didn't know where I was.

I knew I had to get back down to the first floor and

found an escalator going down, but it must not have been the right one. The Pacific cultures exhibit wasn't where I thought it would be, and I wasn't even sure what we'd been looking at when he'd said, "I'll meet you right here." Was it the early musical instruments or the ancient medicine pots? Was it the moccasins made out of reindeer hide or the human skulls? Or was that on the second floor?

Why hadn't I paid attention? First there was that awful empty feeling inside where my heart was thumping like a drum, and then came the dryness that crept up into my throat. Finally my chin began to wobble.

I started blindly down a hall looking for early man, but then I decided I might *really* get lost and had better go back up the escalator and start over, but now I couldn't even find the rest room when I got up there. There were too many people.

A whole class of kids passed by me, all wearing orange T-shirts with SHERWOOD SCHOOL on them. They were laughing and kidding around with each other. *Why can't I be with a bunch of friends,* I thought pitifully, *instead of lost here in the Museum of Natural History with a brother who is probably still looking at medicine pots?* If I had a mother, she never would have let me come downtown with Lester. It would be Mama and me in the Museum of Natural History, and Lester in Air and Space.

I felt tears welling up in my eyes and noticed that the kids from Sherwood School were staring at me and giggling. I whirled around and walked away from them as fast as I could and promptly ran into a group of kindergarten kids in green T-shirts, all holding on to a clothesline, a teacher at the front and the rear.

That's what I needed—a rope! I was a hopeless, helpless Little Girl Lost, who needed a rope to hold on to my life. It was humiliating. Now tears were running down my cheeks.

I saw a security guard over by a drinking fountain, and I walked up to him. "I—I'm l-lost," I said. "Somehow I got s-separated from my brother."

The guard asked my name and then called it into his walkie-talkie. He took me to an escalator, where another guard met me, and this one took me down to a room near the information desk, where two little kids about three or four years old were sitting and crying, snot running down their faces. It was so embarrassing!

It was almost a half hour later when Lester walked in. He didn't see me at first, and his face was pale. But when the guard nodded in my direction and Lester saw me, I couldn't tell if he was more angry or relieved. He walked over and thumped me on the head.

"Knucklehead!" he growled as we went back out into the lobby. "Where *were* you?"

"I got lost, Lester!" I whispered. "I thought it was right

outside in the hall, but it wasn't. And then I realized it was up on the next floor, but when I got there, I—"

"Alice, do you know what I had to *do*?" he said. "I waited and waited, and finally I went to the first rest room I could find and asked a girl to go in there and look for you. She said she checked all the stalls, but nobody fit your description. I was afraid I'd have to try every rest room in the whole museum!"

"I'm sorry, Lester! It was scary!" I whimpered.

He grabbed my hand and gave it a jerk. "Well, *I* was scared too," he said, and jerked it again. At least I knew he loved me.

When we got to the Air and Space Museum, I stuck to Lester like Velcro. When *he* went to the rest room, he made me stand right outside the door, like a dog waiting for his master. I *felt* like a dog.

Lester came out and said, "Well, I'm glad to see you're still here."

"Arf!" I said.

16

Pancakes and Syrup

What happened next was really Lester's fault. He's supposed to get home from school before I do, so I'll never be there by myself. The Wednesday after spring break, some of the kids said they were coming back to the playground after school to watch the skate-boarders. I decided to go back too, so I asked Lester if I could go, and he said it was okay with him. But only a couple of kids showed up, and I didn't even know them. Rosalind didn't come at all, and the sky grew dark. I must have waited fifteen minutes, but when it started to rain, I gave up and went home.

The door was locked, though, and when I rang the bell, nobody came. I pounded on the door, but still Lester didn't come, and I realized he must have gone out. We don't have a porch on our house, and I was really getting wet, so I ran across the yard to the Sheaverses'. They don't have a porch either, and their car was gone.

Boy, Lester, are you ever going to get it! I thought as the rain ran down my back. There wasn't even a toolshed I could hide in! I looked up and down the street. Most of the other cars were gone too, and the few that were left belonged to people I didn't know.

Suddenly I knew what I was going to do. Wrapping my arms around my body and keeping my head down so the rain wouldn't get in my eyes, I went two blocks down the street in the other direction to Megan's house. I went right up the steps and rang the doorbell before I could lose my nerve.

Her little sister answered.

"Hi," I said. "Is Megan here?"

"Yes," said the little girl in the blue overalls, still staring at me. Her eyes looked like two copper pennies.

I heard Megan yell, "Who is it?"

"I don't know. Somebody for you, and she's really wet!" her sister said.

Megan's mouth dropped when she saw me.

"Hi," I said, shivering. "Can I come in?"

She opened the door wider. "What's wrong?" she asked.

"What's wrong," I wanted to say, *"is that we started out on the wrong foot with each other. What's wrong is that we*

seem to be working really hard at being enemies, and I don't think we'd have to work half as hard to be friends."

But what I said was, "My brother went somewhere and locked the door, and I don't have anyplace to go." I stepped inside, dripping water.

Megan could have said, *"Well, why didn't you walk up the street to Rosalind's house?"* But she didn't. What she said was, "Boy, you're really soaked! You want a towel?"

"Okay," I told her.

She brought me a towel, and I blotted my hair with it, then my face and T-shirt. Her little sister kept staring.

"Don't you have a home?" she asked.

Megan and I laughed.

"Yes, but I can't get in," I said. "Now I have to wait till somebody gets there."

"Where's your mother?" asked the sister.

"I don't have a mother," I said. And when the girl looked puzzled, I added, "She died."

Now the sister was really curious. "Did she get killed?" she asked.

"Marlene!" Megan scolded. And then, to me, "You want to wait in the living room?"

"I'd better not sit on anything. I'm too wet," I said.

Megan grinned. "You want to wear some of my clothes?"

I smiled too. "Okay," I said.

We went up to Megan's room, and she found a pair of leggings and a shirt for me. Pretty soon we were sitting on her bed eating cheese crackers.

"Thanks for taking me in," I said. "Lester's really going to catch it."

"Is he your only brother?" she asked.

I nodded. "Is Marlene your only sister?"

"Yep. I don't have any brothers at all."

We chewed for a minute without talking. Then I said, "You could come to my house sometime."

She didn't answer right away. Then, without looking at me, she said, "I didn't think you'd want me to come."

"I guess I didn't think you'd want to. I mean . . . you and Jody and Dawn . . ."

"We're not *really* triplets," she said. "It's just a sort of fun thing to do."

We studied each other and smiled a little.

"Jody would have a fit if she knew I let you in," Megan said.

"Rosalind would have a fit if she knew I *came!*" I said. We both laughed some more. "It's silly to go on being enemies," I said. "It sure is a lot of work."

Megan nodded. "But I think Jody and Dawn sort of like having enemies."

"So?" I said, and waited.

"So why don't we be *secret* friends?" said Megan. "Just until they change their minds."

"Okay," I said.

When it stopped raining, I called home to see if Lester was there yet.

"Yeah?" he said, when he answered.

"Lester, where *were* you?" I asked.

"What do you mean, where was I? I was right here. Where are *you?*"

"You were not! I came home from the playground when it started to rain, and I couldn't get in, and the Sheavers weren't home, and I've probably got pneumonia. I had to go to Megan's."

"You said you were going to the playground."

"I did, but it *rained,* Lester!"

"Well, I was only gone a half hour. I went to Billy's for a new cassette."

"You are in big trouble, Lester!" I said.

"Not if you don't blab, I'm not," he told me.

Megan let me wear her clothes back home when it stopped raining, and I told her I'd bring them back the next afternoon. I didn't tell Dad about Lester, but I did ask for my own key. "What if he gets run over or loses *his* key or something? Then what?" I said.

"Yeah, Dad," said Lester. "You wouldn't want her standing out in the rain with no place to go."

Dad looked us over. "Well, you probably should have your own key, Alice, but I don't like the thought of you losing it on the playground," he said.

"I'll wear it around my neck," I promised.

"And I especially don't like the thought of Lester thinking that maybe it doesn't make any difference whether he's here or not when you get home because you have your own key."

"I'll *be* here!" Lester said. "Only an act of God would keep me away."

An act of God or a new cassette, I told myself. I wonder how God gets blamed for so much stuff.

Dad got our extra house key out of a drawer and found a chain to put it on. I think it was the kind of chain that's attached to the rubber plug in a bathtub, but it was okay with me. I put it around my neck.

"Am I a latchkey kid now?" I asked.

"Not till you're ten," Dad said. "When you're a fifth grader, we'll see how it goes."

When I was in my room later working on my math problems, Lester poked his head in the doorway. "Thanks, Al," he said. "I'll be here from now on. But just in case . . ."

"Just don't blame it on God," I said.

At school the next day, the Terrible Triplets were all wearing purple scrunchies in their hair. But when

Megan passed my desk to go to the pencil sharpener, she winked at me. When I went to use the dictionary near the door, I winked back.

When I got home from school, I put Megan's clothes in a sack and walked to her house. This time she asked me in for some frozen yogurt, and we sat out in the kitchen with her sister, eating it at the table. Her mother was sewing drapes in the dining room and waved to me.

"What's it like having a little sister?" I asked.

"Awful," said Megan, but she smiled at Marlene when she said it. And then, more seriously, she asked, "What's it like not having a mother? Is that awful, too?"

"It's lonely," I said.

"Well, you can come over here anytime you want," she said.

"Yes!" said Marlene. "You can live here if you want to, can't she, Megan?"

Megan and I just laughed.

When Marlene had left the kitchen, though, Megan said, "If we're secret friends, we should each have a code name."

"What should it be?" I asked.

Megan thought about it. "I think I'll make your code name 'Pancakes.'"

I laughed. "Then I'll make yours 'Syrup,'" I said.

17

What Happened at Donald's House

Dad decided it wasn't fair that Lester had to come straight home from school five days a week just to be here for me. So he worked out a deal with Mrs. Sheavers: Donald could have free music lessons at the Melody Inn if I could stay at their house on Tuesdays and Thursdays until Dad got home.

"Wouldn't you like that, Donald? You could learn to play your Uncle Bernie's trumpet!" his mother said happily.

"I don't know," said Donald.

"Is there another instrument you'd rather play?" Dad asked him.

Donald shrugged. "Trumpet's okay, I guess."

Dad studied him for a moment, then said to Mrs. Sheavers, "If he's not really enthusiastic about it, I wouldn't force him."

"Oh, but he *wants* to play the trumpet, don't you, Donald?" she asked brightly.

"I guess so," said Donald. That didn't sound very enthusiastic to me.

"Why don't we try it for a few weeks and see how it goes? Donald can always change his mind," Dad said.

So we had a deal. I wasn't exactly thrilled at having to spend two days a week after school at the Sheaverses'. But at dinner that night, Dad had a little discussion with Lester and me.

"You know," he said, "moving to Maryland is a brand-new experience for us. We've always had your Aunt Sally and Uncle Milt around to help us out, but now we're on our own. We've got to figure things out as they come along. Some will work and some won't, but we'll just have to consider ourselves pioneers on a new frontier."

Dad talks like that sometimes.

"Whatever," said Lester.

The first Tuesday I went home with Donald after school, I told Mrs. Sheavers that Dad said we were pioneers on a new frontier.

Mrs. Sheavers clapped her hands. "And isn't it going to be fun!" she said.

The thing about Donald's mother was that she thought she had to keep Donald and me busy all the time. The minute we got too quiet, she'd poke her head in the room to see what we were doing. And what we were doing was playing Crazy Eights or doing homework, but quiet made her nervous.

When I came home with Donald on Thursday, we found his old red wagon in the center of the living-room floor. On the coffee table, there were long bend-able plastic strips, a big piece of old burlap, and a couple of books on pioneer life. We stared at the wagon and then at Donald's mom.

"Guess what you're going to make!" she said. "A cov-ered wagon!" And when we simply stared some more, she said, "You're the architects! Have fun!" And she went back out in the kitchen.

"Is she always like this?" I asked Donald.

"Only sometimes," said Donald.

So we set to work bending the plastic strips until they formed an arch, then cramming the ends of them down on the inside of the wagon until we had a frame and could stretch the burlap over it.

"Now what?" I said. "Do we have to find a horse?"

"Don't even tell her we're finished. She'll just think of something else," Donald said.

When I came back the following Tuesday, she said we were going to make a sod house. She had the encyclo-pedia opened to pages on the American West, which showed how a sod house was built.

She had a big roll of brown wrapping paper. We were supposed to draw lines on the paper to make it look like blocks of sod, then drape the paper over the dining-room table and cut out a couple of windows.

"Is this dumb or what?" I whispered to Donald. It was like we were back in kindergarten. In nursery school! I wondered what we were going to do next—drag out some old rocking horses and pretend to go riding across the plains?

What bothered me most about Mrs. Sheavers was that I felt she was doing all this to make Dad like her. To make him believe she would be a good mother to me. And all because Dad had said that we were pioneers. Why hadn't I kept my big mouth shut?

While Donald and I wrestled with the wrapping paper and tape, Mrs. Sheavers was out in the kitchen making corn cakes for us to eat in our sod house. We got as far as drawing lines on the paper to look like blocks, but after that, we decided we'd had enough of sod houses for a while and didn't bother to cut out any windows. We just threw a couple of sofa pillows under the dining-room table and crawled under there and told ghost stories.

I told Donald the one Sara had told Rosalind and me about the woman who turned into a praying mantis. Donald told me "The Golden Arm," which I've heard a dozen times already, and I was just in the middle of telling a story that Lester had told me by somebody named Poe, about a man who put his enemy behind a brick wall in his wine cellar, when suddenly an upside-down face appeared in the doorway of the sod house, and Mrs. Sheavers cried, "What are you *doing?*"

I think I must have jumped three inches off the floor. My head fell off the pillow, anyway.

"Just lying here," said Donald.

"Well, you're supposed to be making a sod house!" said his mother.

"It's—it's done," I said, wondering why she was so upset.

"It certainly is not! I don't see any windows in it," she said, and now her face was right side up, and she was down on her knees crawling in the sod house herself. "What's going on?" she asked. "What are these pillows doing in here?"

"We just wanted to lie down," said Donald.

"Why would you want to do that?" asked his mother.

I never heard such stupid questions.

"Because we were tired," I said.

"Why didn't you put any windows in your house?" she said.

I wondered why Donald didn't just answer. Why didn't he tell her the truth? That we were tired of making a stupid sod house out of wrapping paper and would rather tell ghost stories.

But suddenly Mrs. Sheavers crawled out of the sod house again and pulled all the paper off the table. She wadded it up and threw it in the trash can and said we were through playing pioneer.

That was fine with me, but then we smelled something awful. The corn cakes were burning in the kitchen.

At dinner that night, I told Dad what had happened at Donald's house—namely, that *nothing* had happened, and certainly not under the table.

"What's so special about an old sod house made out of paper?" I said. "I didn't even want to play pioneer."

I could tell that Lester was trying not to laugh as he speared his green beans. Dad was smiling too.

"What's wrong with Mrs. Sheavers, anyway?" I asked.

"Just an overactive imagination," said Dad.

I looked at my father as I chewed. "I don't care how many sod houses Mrs. Sheavers makes or how many good ideas she has for keeping me busy. I don't want her for a mother," I said.

"I can promise you that won't happen," said Dad.

At that very moment we heard the most terrible sound coming from next door. At first I thought it was an animal in pain. An elephant, maybe.

"Jeez!" cried Lester. "What's *that*?"

"Donald Sheavers, I'm afraid," said Dad.

"What?" I said.

"Practicing his trumpet," said Dad.

It wasn't much fun going to Donald's on Tuesdays and Thursdays, because Mrs. Sheavers wanted to know what we were doing every minute. As long as we were making noise, it was okay, but every time we did anything quiet, she peeked in on us.

It was a lot of work having to make noise all the time. When we played cards, we bumped our feet against the table legs. When we watched TV, we had to talk during the commercials.

The best times were the days I stopped at our house first and brought Oatmeal over to Donald's. Muffin and Oatmeal loved being together, Donald and I had a good time playing with my cat, and we made enough noise that Mrs. Sheavers wasn't always snooping around.

Near the end of April, there was a cold spell and some of the buds on the bushes froze. I didn't know it was going to be so cold and hadn't worn a jacket to school.

By the time I got to the school driveway, I was freezing. I started to cross, but the patrol girl yelled, "McKinley! Did I tell you to go? Get back over there!" I moved back to the curb, my teeth chattering.

There was no reason in the world why I couldn't cross. The bus that was coming was so far down the block that the whole school could have crossed before it got there, I'll bet. Yet the big patrol girl wouldn't let anyone cross the driveway and made a couple of kindergarten kids wait too.

I was getting colder and colder. Finally the bus came, and the patrol girl moved the orange cones so it could turn in, but she still wouldn't let us cross because another bus, way down the block, was coming from the other direction.

I knew she was punishing me for bumping into her on the playground. As though I'd done it on purpose! But it wasn't just me, it was the kindergarten kids behind me who had to wait too. She was only doing this to show who was boss. My fingers felt almost numb with cold, and I didn't even have pockets to put them in.

I saw Megan standing on the sidewalk across the drive. She gave her head a little toss as if to say, "Come on over! What are you waiting for?"

I nodded toward the patrol girl. Megan rolled her eyes.

I turned and looked at the bus we were supposed to be waiting for. It was still a block away and the light was red. I looked at the patrol girl, whose back was toward us now. I looked at Megan. And suddenly I just stepped down off the curb and walked across the driveway.

The patrol girl turned just then.

"McKinley!" she yelled. "Get back there!"

I kept going.

She put her whistle in her mouth and blew as loud as she could. Then she blew it again. She sounded like a steam engine. My feet didn't stop. I went on over to Megan, who grinned at me, wide-eyed.

"Hey, Pancakes! You're really gutsy!" she said. "That patrol girl would have kept you there all night. I'll bet you're in for it now, though."

"I don't care," I said. "She treats me worse every day."

"Uh-oh. There's Jody. I'd better go," Megan said. "Bye, Pancakes."

"Bye, Syrup," I said, and smiled.

I went inside at the bell. It was sort of fun having a secret friend. Jody and Dawn didn't know we were Pancakes and Syrup, and neither did Rosalind or Sara.

The morning announcements came on over the intercom, the Pledge of Allegiance, and then, for the second time, I heard the principal's voice saying, "Mrs. Burstin, would you send Alice McKinley to my office, please?"

18

Spring Thaw

Before we moved to Takoma Park, I'd never in my eight years of life been sent to the principal's office. And now I was going for the second time! My mouth was so dry, it felt like there was a sock in it. I knew right away that the big patrol girl had reported me.

I imagined telling Dad that night that I'd had to go see Mr. Serio. That I'd disobeyed the patrol girl on purpose. Sure enough, when I got to the office, the secretary pointed me toward the door at the back, and as I went in, the patrol girl came out with a grin as wide as a ruler on her face.

"You're in for it now, McKinley," she whispered as we passed in the doorway.

I wanted to grab her face in my hand and just scrunch it up.

But then I was standing in Mr. Serio's office, looking at the tall, thin man who was sitting behind his desk. His tie had little red, white, and blue figures on it, but they weren't flags or anything. They were tiny little Snoopy dogs turned in different directions. I figured that any man who wore a Snoopy tie probably wouldn't lock me in a broom closet or anything.

"Well, hello again, Alice," he said, motioning me to a chair. "Have a seat, will you?" His voice was polite enough, but he wasn't smiling. "I think you've been here long enough now to know our rules, and obeying the safety patrols is one of them."

My lips seemed frozen shut. The Snoopy tie hadn't helped as much as I thought it would.

"Ruby tells me that you crossed the driveway in spite of her telling you to go back, and even when she blew her whistle, you went ahead."

The patrol girl had a name: Ruby.

Mr. Serio went on. "It's hard for me to believe you'd do that, because I haven't had any bad reports about you from Mrs. Burstin. So what happened?"

I opened my mouth, but my lips stuck together for a moment, they were that dry. "I did cross the driveway because she always makes me wait longer than anybody. When there's a bus coming two blocks away, she still makes me wait, and it's not fair."

My heart was beating so hard, I looked down to see if it was thumping through my T-shirt.

"I know that it can seem a very long time when you're waiting to cross—" he began, but I interrupted.

"She hates me because I bumped into her once on the playground by accident and we both fell down. This morning she made me wait for two buses, and the second one was blocks away."

"Ruby did! I saw it too!" came a voice behind me, and I saw Megan standing in the doorway. The school secretary was coming up behind her, ready to snatch her away.

Mr. Serio stared at Megan. So did I.

"And what's your name?"

"Megan Beachy. I was on the other side of the drive-way, and it's just like Alice said."

I couldn't believe Megan was there. That she would do this for me.

"Well, I'll have a talk with Ruby," Mr. Serio said. "But meanwhile, we can't have students disobeying the patrols, Alice. It's especially important when younger children are watching. You understand that."

I nodded.

"You too, Megan?" asked Mr. Serio.

"Yes," she said.

"All right. You girls get back to class. And, Megan,

when I want you to come to the office, I'll let you know, okay?"

"Okay," she said.

Out in the hall, I grabbed her hand. "Did you sneak out of class, or what?" I asked.

"When I heard Mr. Serio call for you, I figured Ruby had told. So I asked to go to the rest room and came here instead. We can't let her get away with that."

"Thanks, Syrup," I whispered.

"Anytime, Pancakes," she said.

My dad and I have never had secrets, and even though Mr. Serio didn't send a note home or anything, I began to feel worse and worse that I hadn't told him I had been called to the principal's office the first time.

So that night at dinner, while we were eating our tacos, I said, "I got called to the principal's office, Dad." Then I swallowed and said, "For the second time."

Dad and Lester both looked at me.

"Alice!" Dad said, surprised. "What on Earth for?"

"Different reasons," I said.

"And . . . ?" Dad put down his taco, but Lester went right on eating.

"Well, today it was because I crossed the driveway before the safety patrol girl said I could, and she reported me."

"Oh." Dad picked up his taco again, but he didn't eat it. "And why did you do that?"

"Because she was making me wait on purpose. She hates my guts, and I was cold! But Megan heard Mr. Serio announce my name, and she came to the office too, and she said I was right—that Ruby makes me wait for no reason."

"And what did Mr. Serio say?"

"That he'll talk to Ruby." I thought about how I was making it all sound like Ruby's fault, and I wanted Dad to know that I realized this was serious. "And that if I cross the driveway in front of kindergarten kids when I'm not supposed to, they could follow after me and get run over."

"Well, that's right, Alice. I'm glad you see his point."

"So what got you called to the principal's office the first time?" Lester said, wishing for a little more excitement, I guess. He got it.

I kept my eyes on my plate. "I told everybody that Uncle Charlie was murdered."

"You *what?*" Dad yelped, and this time he dropped his taco. A bean bounced off the edge of the table. Even Lester stopped chewing.

"Well . . . he—he didn't kill himself," I said.

"What does *that* have to do with anything?" asked Dad.

I started to cry. My voice got tight and high, and I

sounded like Oatmeal's mew when we first got her: "W-When we got back from T-Tennessee, everyone was t-teasing me about being on a honeymoon with Donald Sheavers, and I had to make them s-stop. So I—I told them that—that Uncle Charlie got murdered."

Lester was staring as though I had just sprouted two heads.

"But *why* would you tell them that?" Dad exclaimed.

"S-So we could talk about something else besides honeymoons and kissing."

"It wouldn't be enough to just tell them Charlie died?" he asked.

"That would have made me cry," I said, and cried all the harder.

"Well," Lester said, "you have to admit she's creative, Dad."

Dad didn't look quite as angry as he had before. He just studied me for a while, and then he asked, "How did Mr. Serio find out what you were telling everyone?"

"I don't know," I sniffled. "I guess he heard the kids talking."

"Do they still think your uncle was murdered?"

"I don't know," I said in a tiny little voice. "I told them the police are investigating."

Dad pushed his plate away from him and rested his hands on the table. "Sometimes, Alice, I just don't know what to do with you."

I started bawling all over again.

But suddenly Lester was standing up for me. "You know what this is, Dad? It's the 'new kid' syndrome. Alice is new in school this year and kids are picking on her, and she's trying to deal with it the best she can."

Dad's shoulders slumped a little, but this time he smiled. "Okay, Al, but can you possibly keep out of the principal's office for the rest of the year? Can you at least try?"

That much I could promise. "I promise to try," I said, wiping my eyes with my sleeve.

A week later it was my turn to do something for Megan. I got to school about fifteen minutes early, and some of the fifth-grade boys had started a baseball game. They were using one guy's jacket for third base, a piece of cardboard for second, and Megan's backpack for first.

When I walked up to where the Terrible Triplets were standing, I could see that Megan was trying not to cry.

"They grabbed it right out of my hands," she said. "They didn't even ask."

"You give that back!" Jody shouted at the boys.

"Relax! We just borrowed it!" the pitcher yelled. He threw the ball again; the batter hit it and went tearing over to first base, where he landed on the backpack and sent it skidding along in the dirt.

"Safe!" somebody yelled.

All the boys were cheering as the next one got up to bat. The first runner was standing with one foot on Megan's backpack, ready to run to second base the first chance he got, and when the batter sent the ball flying, the first runner made it to second. The boy who hit the ball went racing over to first, jumped on the backpack, then made it to second. All the boys were shouting.

"They're ruining it!" Dawn cried.

The third batter missed the first pitch. He missed a second one, too. But when the pitcher threw the ball again, he hit it and ran to first, and the minute he started for second, I raced onto the field, almost colliding with the boy who was running to home base, grabbed Megan's backpack, and went running back to her as all the boys yelled at me. All four of us, Megan and Jody and Dawn and I, ran to the school steps and stood panting there by the door, waiting to catch our breath.

The backpack was a mess.

When Megan unzipped it, the books were okay, but her notebook had come apart and her lunch was totally squashed.

"I guess I should have got it sooner," I said. Dawn and Jody were staring at me. The bell rang then and we all went inside, but as soon as I got to my desk, Rosalind came over.

"What were you doing with *them?*" she asked.

"Just rescuing a backpack," I said.

"They wouldn't have done it for you," she said.

"You never know," I told her.

Later, as Megan passed by my desk, she dropped a tiny scrap of paper all folded up into a tiny square. When no one was looking, I unfolded it. *Thanks, Pancakes!* it read.

Around the first of May, the Naked Nomads met in our basement again, and Rosalind came along. We invited Sara too, and while all the noise was going on in the basement, the three of us sat on my bed with a big bowl of popcorn to make plans. I knew what I wanted to say, but I wasn't sure how to say it.

"You know," I said at last, when I was sure both Rosalind and Sara had a mouthful of popcorn and couldn't interrupt me for a few seconds, "it's always the same with the Terrible Triplets. Why don't we do something they couldn't possibly expect?"

"Like dump water on them?" said Rosalind.

"Something they *really* wouldn't expect," I said.

"Be nice to them?" said Sara.

"Close," I said. "Invite them to my birthday party."

Rosalind just stared.

"When's your birthday?" asked Sara.

"May fourteenth."

"Are you crazy?" said Rosalind. "After all the work we've done to show them how stuck-up they are, we're going to invite them to a *party?*"

"That's just what I mean," I said. "Look how hard we work to keep on being enemies. They don't have to be our 'best' friends, but why couldn't they just be ordinary, everyday friends?"

I could tell she didn't think much of the idea. "Because they act stupid, trying to be triplets and everything," she said.

"But maybe they wouldn't act so bad if we were nicer," said Sara.

"Yeah," I said. "If they don't come to the party and go on being stuck-up, well, at least we tried. I don't want to start fourth grade next fall with the same people hoping I'll break my neck on the monkey bars or something. I've already got Ruby mad at me."

"Who's Ruby?"

"The big patrol girl in fifth," I said.

"Did your dad say you could have a party?" Sara asked.

"He said I could invite as many people as I am old. So I get to have nine people, counting myself."

"So who are you going to invite?" asked Rosalind. "The three of us, the Terrible Triplets, that's six . . ."

"There's just one problem," I added. "Dad says I have to invite Donald Sheavers."

"A *boy?*" screeched Rosalind and Sara together.

"Because he lives next door and his mom takes care of me after school on Tuesdays and Thursdays," I explained.

"Who ever heard of a boy at a girl's birthday party?" Rosalind said.

"I thought I'd tell Donald he could invite two other boys from our class. Then there would be three of everything—three of us, the three Triplets, and three boys. Maybe the boys will act crazy enough that we won't have to sit and glare at Jody and Dawn and Megan all evening."

"What if the Triplets don't show?" said Rosalind.

"They'll come," I said confidently, thinking that Megan would persuade them to come.

"And if they don't," Sara said, grinning, "that's all the more cake and ice cream for us!"

It was risky business, I knew. I hadn't made a very good start in third grade, but now that spring was here and everything was starting to bloom, it just seemed like a good time for change. On Monday, I sent invitations to Jody, Dawn, Megan, Sara, and Rosalind, and I took one next door to Donald and told him to invite two more boys from our class, I didn't care who.

"Okay," said Donald.

That Friday I still didn't know whether anyone had received the invitations yet or not. I was thinking about the party when I suddenly heard someone yell, "Stop right there, McKinley!"

I realized I had stepped off the curb without waiting for the go-ahead from Ruby. I froze, one foot in the air, and then stepped back on the curb. Ruby turned her back to me then, probably hoping I'd try to sneak across so she could report me again. She looked up and down the street. It seemed to take her a long time to figure out that no bus was coming, but finally she turned back to me.

"Okay, McKinley, you can go," she said.

"Mother-May-I?" I said.

Ruby stared at me a moment, but I was smiling.

"Yes, you may," she said, and it almost looked like she was smiling too.

I crossed the drive taking scissor steps, as though we were playing a game. And Ruby actually laughed out loud. Was it possible that even Ruby and I could be friends?

I went inside to our room, and when Megan saw me, she gave me the thumbs-up sign. That must have meant that Dawn and Jody had talked it over and decided to come to my party. I *knew* that Sara and Rosalind would come.

"What about you, Donald? Have you picked two other boys for my party?" I asked.

"Not yet," said Donald.

I began to wonder if inviting Donald would turn out to be a really huge mistake.

19

The Party

The day of my ninth birthday party, I still didn't know who Donald was going to bring. Dad began to wish he hadn't said I could invite as many people as I had. "Once you turn ten," he said, "that's the limit."

"I don't think there should be more than three," said Lester.

"Three!" I cried. "Why three?"

"You, me, and Dad," said Lester.

An hour before the kids came, I took a bath and put some gardenia bubble soap in the water. I washed my hair and combed it. I chose white tights, a green-and-white-checked skirt, and a short-sleeved green top, with tiny pearl buttons down the front. I wished I had some perfume. How could it be, I wondered, that I was nine years old now and still didn't have any perfume or cologne?

I went in Dad's bedroom and looked on his dresser. I found a bottle of Calvin Klein cologne. I took the cap off and stuck my finger all the way inside until my whole finger felt wet. Then I wiped it across my forehead, down each cheek, across my chin, behind each ear, and under my elbows.

I put on my black shoes with the shiny bows and went in the living room to show Lester how beautiful I looked.

"Whew!" he said. "It smells like the Kiwanis Club just walked in here. What have you got on, Alice?"

"Just some cologne," I said.

"It must be Dad's. You've put on men's cologne!"

I stared. "You mean there are men's cologne *and* women's cologne?"

"Of course."

"And they smell different?"

"Sure do."

"How is a man's smell different from a woman's?"

"I don't know, it just is. Women's perfumes are more like flowers and fruit, I guess, and men's are more like animals."

What Lester was trying to tell me, I guess, was that I smelled like a skunk.

I went in the bathroom, took a washcloth, and

washed my forehead, my cheeks, my chin, behind my ears, and under my elbows. Then I went out in the kitchen and stuck my finger in a carton of orange juice. I wiped my wet finger across my forehead, down each cheek, across my chin, behind each ear, and under each elbow.

"Are you ready, Alice?" Dad called from the other room. "I think I see some of your friends arriving."

I ran to the window and looked. There were Jody and Dawn getting out of a car. *No, not them!* I thought. I didn't want them to be the first! What was I going to say with nobody else around?

"Dad!" I cried. "It's Jody and Dawn! What am I going to do?"

"You're going to open the door and say, 'Come in,'" said Dad. So that's what I did.

"Hi, Dawn. Hi, Jody. Come in," I said.

"Happy birthday," they both said, and each handed me a present.

I had a sudden, horrible feeling it would be dog doo. A terrible feeling that I would open their gifts in front of everybody, and it would be something so awful that it would make everyone sick. Like a frog's intestines, maybe, and Jody would say, "That's what we think of *you!*" and walk out.

But just then Donald came over from next door, and I saw Megan coming up the sidewalk, and pretty soon

Sara arrived with her hair freshly washed and combed, and then Rosalind. Finally the two boys came that Donald Sheavers had invited: Ollie Harris and . . . Cory Schwartz!

"Not Cory Schwartz!" I wanted to scream. This party was going to be a disaster. This party was going to be awful!

The boys wouldn't even come into the living room. They just set the presents they had brought on the floor in the hallway, and then they started to whisper and laugh and punch one another, as all the girls tried to squeeze together on the couch. I went out in the kitchen to get Dad. *Maybe I should just keep walking,* I thought. *Maybe I should go straight through the kitchen and on out the back door and keep going and not stop until I got to Delaware.*

"Dad!" I said. "What are we going to do now?"

"Maybe you should play a game," he said.

But all the games I'd thought of seemed dumb. I didn't think anyone wanted to play a game right then. My neck itched, and wherever I scratched, it felt sticky. The orange juice! I had to wash off the orange juice. I grabbed a paper towel and put it under the faucet, then rubbed my face and neck and arms.

Suddenly I heard a lot of ahs and ohs, and I went back out in the living room. Oatmeal had walked into the room, and the girls had scooped her up in their arms and were passing her from one person to the next. The boys had got as far as the doorway to the living room and were calling to the cat and trying to get her to come over to them.

I sat down on the floor with a piece of string. I pulled it along the rug, and Oatmeal leaped off the couch and crouched down, her back legs tense, her pupils huge, ready to spring. Everyone laughed.

Somehow it was easier after that. Once we had the kitten to watch, we didn't have to sit and look at each other. Megan put her present down on the floor beside me, and I took off the ribbon. I dangled it above Oatmeal's head and let her jump at it.

Inside the box was a little red heart made out of glass. I think it was a paperweight.

"Thank you, Megan," I said, and we gave each other our secret wink.

I opened Jody and Dawn's gifts next. Glass-bead bracelets—a pink one from Dawn, a green one from Jody. Sara gave me a book on volcanoes, and Rosalind gave me a box of caramels.

It was the boys' presents that were sort of weird. I got a model airplane and some glue from Donald, a comic book from Ollie, and a key chain with a little seal on it from Cory. The seal had a hat on its head with X's on it, and Donald said the X's stood for kisses, and that made Donald and Ollie hoot and holler and the girls giggle, and then the boys wrestled around on the floor with Cory, and Dad said, "Okay, everybody. Downstairs!"

I guess he figured that if we were going to destroy the furniture, it had better be Lester's. So everyone got up and followed Dad and Lester to the basement.

Of course, what the boys noticed right away was Lester's drum set, and they all wanted to try it out. Lester said they couldn't fool around with it alone, but he'd give each of them a turn.

So he put on a cassette and showed Donald and Cory and Ollie how to use the pedal for the bass drum and the sticks for the tom-toms. While the guys were drumming, Megan and Dawn and Jody started dancing to the music, and then Megan taught me one of the steps and Dawn and Jody taught Sara and Rosalind.

The surprising thing was, Rosalind caught on to the dance step quicker than anyone else. Her feet just seemed to know what to do, and when Jody took her hand and held it up in the air, Rosalind made a turnaround underneath, just like she'd been dancing all her life. Maybe, up in her room, all by herself, she had. That's the way it is with friends, I guess. You think you know everything about them, and then they surprise you.

We danced until we got sweaty, and suddenly I realized that we were having a good time—we were laughing and kidding around, and pretty soon the girls got their turns on the drums. Jody tried to get Cory to dance with her, but he wouldn't.

We went back upstairs for cake and ice cream, and Sara asked if we could give Oatmeal some ice cream too. Dad said no, you really shouldn't give cats much cream, but we could let her lick our bowls when we were finished.

So everyone started setting their empty bowls on the floor after the ice cream was gone, and I went to get Oatmeal.

"Where is she, Dad?" I called.

"Isn't she there with you? Did you look behind the couch?" he said.

Cory and Donald looked behind the couch and we checked under the other chairs, but the kitten wasn't there.

I went in my room and looked under the bed. In my closet, where Oatmeal sometimes sleeps on my dirty clothes. I checked Dad's room, too. She wasn't there.

"Rosalind," I said, and I could feel my lips begin to quiver, "I can't find Oatmeal."

We all started looking then. We looked under the sofa pillows and on the dining-room chairs, and then we went back to the basement to see if the kitten was there. It was right then that I saw that someone had propped open the basement door a few inches, the door that leads out into the backyard. It had gotten warm in the basement while we were dancing, and I guess someone decided to let in some air.

I'd forgotten to tell my friends that Oatmeal was an indoor cat—that we never let her out.

Lester came downstairs with his headphones on, but when he saw us swarming around the basement, he took the headphones off.

"What's wrong?" he asked.

"Oatmeal," I said. "She got out, I think. Somebody propped open the basement door."

"I didn't know she wasn't supposed to get out," said Ollie. "I just didn't know that."

"I forgot to tell you," I said, hoping I wouldn't cry.

"We'll make a search party!" said Jody. "We'll all go out and look for her."

"She—she doesn't know about cars or anything." I gulped, trying not to let the tears slide out of my eyes. "If she met up with a dog, it could kill her."

Lester slipped on his shoes. "I'll come too," he said. "Where did you see her last?"

"I think she was coming down the basement stairs when we started dancing," Dawn said.

"I saw her when I was playing the drums," Cory said.

Jody was the first one out the basement door, and the rest of us followed. How could a party that had been going so well turn out so badly? I wondered. If anything happened to Oatmeal, it would be one of the worst birthdays I'd ever had.

And yet, outside, it was a beautiful May night. Dad always said it had been beautiful the night I was born, too. He said it was just the right kind of night for bringing a new baby girl into the world. Why couldn't it be that kind of a happy night right now?

We scattered over the backyard; the others called, "Oatmeal! Oatmeal!" while I called, "Here, kitty-kitty-kitty," in the high kind of voice that usually brought Oatmeal running. We didn't see her, though.

I grabbed hold of Lester's hand in the darkness, and he gripped my fingers as we walked across the wet grass toward the street. I didn't think I could stand it if I saw that Oatmeal had been run over. I'd cry in front of everyone, I knew it.

The girls looked behind all the bushes in the yard, and the boys checked behind the trash cans in the alley. If Oatmeal had wandered away, she'd probably never find her way home again. If anyone found such a cute little kitten, they'd probably keep her. I fought back tears again.

"I'm going to get Killer and see if he can help," said Donald.

"Killer?" cried Dawn.

"His real name is Muffin, but we call him Killer just for fun," Donald said.

We waited till Donald came back with his dog on a leash.

"That's a dog?" said Cory. "He looks more like a mop."

"He looks a hundred years old!" said Sara.

"He is, in dog years, but Oatmeal loves him," said Donald.

"Oatmeal and Muffin," said Jody.

"Just like Pancakes and Syrup," Megan whispered to me.

"Why don't we start across all the backyards on the block?" Lester suggested. "Since Oatmeal's outside for the first time, she might stay away from a noisy street. My guess is she'll be exploring around the neighbors' bushes."

So we formed a line and started across Donald's backyard, with a circle of light from Lester's flashlight pointing the way.

"Hey, this is cool!" I heard Ollie say. "It's like a night rescue. We should have infrared glasses so we could see in the dark."

"I'll bet that dog of yours can't even see," said Jody to Donald.

"He can't," said Donald. "But his nose still works."

Muffin was walking up ahead, Donald holding on to the leash. We crossed one neighbor's yard, then another. All at once the dog's tail began to wag. Then he began to walk a little faster. He almost began to trot.

He went right over to a lilac bush beneath a window, and when Lester turned the beam of light on Muffin, we saw a gray-and-white kitten come out from under the bushes and rub up against Muffin's leg.

"There she is!" everyone cried.

"Oatmeal!" I called, and scooped my little kitten up in my nine-year-old arms. Everyone crowded around, talking to her, saying what a naughty little cat she was, patting her on the head.

We walked back to our house with Lester, following the beam of his flashlight. The air had a sweet smell, like a touch of honey, and Oatmeal felt like a powder puff in my arms, a little purring bundle of fluff.

I felt like purring too. I think that deep down, where no one could hear it, I *was* purring. It was my ninth birthday, and nine friends—counting Lester—were celebrating with me. They weren't all "best" friends— maybe only a few—but you don't have to be best friends just to like someone.

We were making a new start on a new street in a new state, and Oatmeal was back in my arms. I couldn't wait to get home and tell Dad. And for the first time, Lester reached over to pet my kitten.

What's next for Alice in third grade?
Here's a sneak preview from

Alice in Blunderland.

Being Perfect

Lester lies to me sometimes, only he says it's just teasing. Then I go and believe him.

We were talking about names once, and he said he'd let me in on a secret if I didn't tell Dad. He said that we weren't Scotch-Irish at all, that our grandparents had escaped from Russia, but we didn't want anyone to know it.

My real name, he said, wasn't Alice Kathleen McKinley; it was Alicia Katerina de Balencia Blunderbuss Makinoli.

"Honest?" I said.

"Cross my heart," said Lester.

"Write it down," I told him. So Lester wrote it down for me.

I whispered my real name over and over so I could remember it. That night at the dinner table I watched my dad eat his green beans and wondered what other secrets he was keeping from me.

"What's Dad's real name then?" I asked Lester later.

"Hmm," said Lester. "That's a hard one to remember. It's Ivan Ilvonovich Rostropovich."

"I thought you said our last name was Makinoli."

"Right! Ivan Ilvonovich Rostropovich Makinoli."

"Then what's *your* real name?" I asked.

"Dmitri Rachmaninoff Schvaglio Deuteronomy Makinoli," said Lester.

I studied my brother. "Honest?" I asked.

"Would I lie to you?" said Lester.

"Honest *honest*?"

"Cross my heart," said Lester. "But it's a secret, and Dad's sort of touchy about it. He'll get around to telling you sometime."

The next day at school I couldn't help myself. Instead of writing Alice McKinley at the top of my fourth-grade spelling paper, I wrote Alicia

Katerina de Balencia Blunderbuss Makinoli.

When we traded papers with the person beside us for checking, my friend Rosalind said, "What's this?" and pointed to the name at the top.

I thumped my chest. "Me," I said. "I just found out."

Rosalind looked at the name again. "Are you sure that last name isn't supposed to be Macaroni?"

"No," I said. "It's not."

Rosalind got up and went to the dictionary. When she came back, she said, "Do you know what a blunderbuss is?"

"No," I said.

"A person who goofs up," said Rosalind.

"Lester!" I yelled when I walked in the house that afternoon. My brother is about seven and a half years older than me, and he gets home from high school before grade school even lets out. "You just stuck 'Blunderbuss' in there. That's not part of my real name at all!"

"Imagine that!" said Lester.

"I'll bet you made that whole thing up," I said.

"How'd you guess?" said Lester.

I don't know why Lester couldn't have been a girl. Why couldn't I have had an older sister instead, one who would show me how to braid my hair and sew on a button and make fudge and cut my toenails?

My mother died when I was in kindergarten, and Lester and I live in Takoma Park, Maryland, with our dad, Ben McKinley. We moved here last year from Chicago. So instead of a big sister who could braid my hair, I've got a brother who plays the drums in a band called the Naked Nomads and tells me lies. I've got a cat, though, named Oatmeal, and that's our family—me and Dad and Lester and Oatmeal.

The fact is—and that's why Lester made me angry, I guess—I really am a blunderbuss. Fourth grade is definitely the worst. I have already made more embarrassing mistakes in the fourth grade than in all the other grades put together.

Last Sunday, Dad took me to the mall and I had to go to the restroom. After I flushed, I tried to open the door of my stall, but I couldn't get it unlocked. I pushed and pulled, but the metal bar wouldn't slide. My father was waiting outside, but I would be stuck in there forever, I thought! They would have to feed me through the space under the door! I was too embarrassed to yell. Too embarrassed to pound on the door.

I could hear three women talking at the sink, and I decided I would wait until they had gone. Then I would crawl out under the door. I heard the women go out. I heard their voices fade away. Then I got down beside the toilet and crawled out underneath the door. There was still a woman left at the sink.

She gave a little gasp and turned around. I think she thought I was a dog.

"Hello," I said as I washed my hands.

She just stared.

On Monday, Sara, my second best friend, wanted to borrow a piece of paper at school. I handed her one. I had been eating a Hershey's candy bar the night before when I did my homework. There was chocolate on the paper.

"Euuuw!" said Sara, handing it back. "What's this? Poop?"

Everybody looked at me and laughed. I'll bet my face was as red as Sara's T-shirt.

On Tuesday we were eating beans and franks in the lunchroom. My mouth was full, and suddenly I sneezed. I sent beans and franks flying all over Megan's tray. "Euuuw!" said Megan, and she dumped her tray in the trash can.

Wednesday night it rained. I was in the bathtub when I heard raindrops pattering down on our roof. And right that minute I remembered that I had left my geography book on the front steps. It would be ruined!

I leaped out of the bathtub and pulled on my underpants. It was dark outside, so I ran to the front door, slipped out on the porch, and grabbed up the book. And there was Donald Sheavers from next door, taking trash to the garbage can. He saw. *He* says my name is Alice Kathleen Underpants McKinley.

Fourth grade stinks. Fourth grade is when everything you do embarrasses you. Fourth grade is when everyone knows you're a blunderbuss whether it's part of your name or not.

One morning at breakfast I said to my dad, "I'm going to try to go the rest of my life without doing any more embarrassing things. I won't do anything unless I think about it first."

"Good luck," said Lester.

"That doesn't sound like much of a life to me," said Dad.

"Why not?" I asked, my mouth full of scrambled egg.

"Because if you have to stop and think before you do anything, you'll never do anything spontaneous at all."

It seemed like more fun than being a blunderbuss.

Donald Sheavers came over to walk to school with me. He always stands with his nose pressed against the back screen until Dad invites him in. Then he sits and plays with Oatmeal till I finish my breakfast.

Oatmeal is a gray-and-white cat. The only things she does are eat and sleep and play and poop and pee. If you laugh at a cat because she does something funny, she'll just do it again. Cats don't get embarrassed, even when they throw up.

"I should have been born a cat," I told Donald Sheavers on the way to school.

"You might get worms," said Donald.

"Not if I lived inside," I said.

"You might get fleas," said Donald.

"Not if I never went out," I told him.

"You might get run over," said Donald.

"Not if I stayed in the house," I said.

"So who wants to live like that?" said Donald.

We have a man teacher in fourth grade. His name is Mr. Dooley. Out on the playground some of the kids call him "Mr. Dodo" or "Mr. Doo-bee" or "Mr. Doo-doo," but he just smiles. We've only been in his classroom for two weeks, but Mr. Dooley never seems to get angry. Donald says if you set fire to Mr. Dooley's pants, he still wouldn't get mad.

He's not a blunderbuss, either. He never seems to make mistakes. He doesn't spill food on his shirts or forget our names or lose his attendance book or squeak the chalk on the blackboard. I guess he's as perfect as a teacher can be.

I decided I wanted to be like Mr. Dooley. Even if kids made fun of me, I would just laugh.

Mr. Dooley thinks *we* are the weird ones. He says fourth grade is a zoo. Except for Donald Sheavers and me walking to school together every morning, the boys and girls in fourth grade keep away from each other.

Mr. Dooley says boys and girls our age are like salt and pepper. He says we are like north and south. He says we are like magnetic poles that repel each other. He says he likes teaching fourth grade.

But one day Mr. Dooley's car wouldn't start, and he was late getting to school. The principal had to come down to our room and take over until he got there. And I could tell that Mr. Dooley had a headache when he came in. His eyes were sort of squinting, and his eyebrows came together over the top of his nose.

"Donald, either sit on your chair the way it was intended or put it on your head," he snapped.

Donald put his chair on his head, and Mr. Dooley sent him to the back of the room.

There was a special guest in school that day who was going to talk about her books. We were going to be studying one of them in our class, and Mr. Dooley had been reading it aloud.

We were very lucky to have an author visit our school, Mr. Dooley said. When we joined the fifth graders in the all-purpose room, he wanted us to be on our best behavior. He wanted us to show them that we could be just as grown up as they were. I wondered if Mr. Dooley had ever taught fifth graders. Out on the playground they didn't seem very grown up to me.

We are never on our best behavior just before lunch because we're getting hungry. We were joking and laughing as we followed Mr. Dooley down the hall to where the author was waiting. As we giggled and pushed our way into the all-purpose room, the fifth graders looking at us, Mr. Dooley suddenly yelled, "If you don't settle down, I'm going to seat you boy-girl-boy-girl."

We were so quiet then that we could even hear Mr. Dooley's stomach growl as we passed him in the doorway. It was a loud gurgling rumble. We almost laughed, but didn't. We were so quiet, we could hear our own breathing.

The author smiled at us and thanked us for being quiet. She said she had written thirteen books and wanted to tell us about them. And then she did the most amazing thing. She accidentally burped, right into the microphone. Mr. Dooley may not have had any breakfast that morning because of his car, but I'll bet the author had eaten a very big breakfast because it was an awfully loud burp. Everybody laughed, even the fifth graders.

The author looked embarrassed. Mr. Dooley looked embarrassed for her. I felt horrible too. If teachers' stomachs growled in public and authors burped into microphones, this meant I would probably keep right on doing embarrassing things, too, for the rest of my life.

PHYLLIS REYNOLDS NAYLOR

STARTING WITH ALICE
Atheneum Books for
  Young Readers
  0-689-84395-X
Aladdin Paperbacks
  0-689-84396-8

ALICE IN BLUNDERLAND
Atheneum Books for
  Young Readers
  0-689-84397-6
Aladdin Paperbacks
  0-689-84398-4

LOVINGLY ALICE
Atheneum Books for
  Young Readers
  0-689-84399-2
Aladdin Paperbacks
  0-689-84400-X

THE AGONY OF ALICE
Atheneum Books for
  Young Readers
  0-689-31143-5
Aladdin Paperbacks
  0-689-81672-3

ALICE IN RAPTURE,
  SORT-OF
Atheneum Books for
  Young Readers
  0-689-31466-3
Aladdin Paperbacks
  0-689-81687-1

RELUCTANTLY ALICE
Atheneum Books for
  Young Readers
  0-689-31681-X
Aladdin Paperbacks
  0-689-81688-X

ALL BUT ALICE
Atheneum Books for
Young Readers
  0-689-31773-5
Aladdin Paperbacks
  0-689-85044-1

ALICE IN APRIL
Atheneum Books for
  Young Readers
  0-689-31805-7
Aladdin Paperbacks
  0-689-81686-3

ALICE IN-BETWEEN
Atheneum Books for
  Young Readers
  0-689-31890-0
Aladdin Paperbacks
  0-689-81685-5

ALICE THE BRAVE
Atheneum Books for
  Young Readers
  0-689-80095-9
Aladdin Paperbacks
  0-689-80598-5

ALICE IN LACE
Atheneum Books for
  Young Readers
  0-689-80358-3
Aladdin Paperbacks
  0-689-80597-7

OUTRAGEOUSLY ALICE
Atheneum Books for
  Young Readers
  0-689-80354-0
Aladdin Paperbacks
  0-689-80596-9

ACHINGLY ALICE
Atheneum Books for
  Young Readers
  0-689-80533-9
Aladdin Paperbacks
  0-689-80595-0
Simon Pulse
  0-689-86396-9

ALICE ON THE OUTSIDE
Atheneum Books for
  Young Readers
  0-689-80359-1
Simon Pulse
  0-689-80594-2

GROOMING OF ALICE
Atheneum Books for
  Young Readers
  0-689-82633-8
Simon Pulse
  0-689-84618-5

ALICE ALONE
Atheneum Books for
  Young Readers
  0-689-82634-6
Simon Pulse
  0-689-85189-8

SIMPLY ALICE
Atheneum Books for
  Young Readers
  0-689-84751-3
Simon Pulse
  0-689-85965-1

PATIENTLY ALICE
Atheneum Books for
  Young Readers
  0-689-82636-2
Simon Pulse
  0-689-87073-6

INCLUDING ALICE
Atheneum Books for
  Young Readers
  0-689-82637-0
Simon Pulse
  0-689-87074-4

ALICE ON HER WAY
Atheneum Books for
  Young Readers
  0-689-87090-6

ALICE IN THE KNOW
Atheneum Books for
  Young Readers
  0-689-87092-2

PHYLLIS REYNOLDS NAYLOR'S

SHILOH

TRILOGY

The beloved classic saga of a boy and his dog

Atheneum
0-689-31914-3

Aladdin Paperbacks
0-689-83582-5

Aladdin movie tie-in
0-689-83583-3

**Newbery Medal
Winner**

**American Library
Association Notable
Children's Book**

**International Reading
Association Teachers'
Choice**

**International Reading
Association Young
Adult Choice**

Atheneum
0-689-80647-7

Aladdin
0-689-80646-9

Aladdin video tie-in
0-689-82931-0

***Booklist* Editors'
Choice**

Atheneum
0-689-81460-7

Aladdin Paperbacks
0-689-81461-5

Aladdin Paperbacks
0-689-01525-9

Simon & Schuster Children's
Publishing Division